The Visitor

The Visitor

Christopher Chase Walker

COSMIC
EGG
BOOKS

Winchester, UK
Washington, USA

First published by Cosmic Egg Books, 2016
Cosmic Egg Books is an imprint of John Hunt Publishing Ltd., Laurel House, Station Approach,
Alresford, Hants, SO24 9JH, UK
office1@jhpbooks.net
www.johnhuntpublishing.com

For distributor details and how to order please visit the 'Ordering' section on our website.

Text copyright: Christopher Chase Walker 2015

ISBN: 978 1 78535 535 6
978 1 78535 536 3 (ebook)
Library of Congress Control Number: 2016943149

A CIP catalogue record for this book is available from the British Library.

Design: Stuart Davies

Printed and bound by CPI Group (UK) Ltd, Croydon, CR0 4YY, UK

We operate a distinctive and ethical publishing philosophy in all
areas of our business, from our global network of authors to
production and worldwide distribution.

To Mary

If chance with nymphlike step fair virgin pass,
What pleasing seemed, for her now pleases more,
She most, and in her looks sums all delight:
Such pleasure took the Serpent to behold
This flowery plat, the sweet recess of Eve
Thus early, thus alone; her sweet heavenly form
Angelic, but more soft and feminine,
Her graceful innocence, her every air
Of gesture or least action, overawed
His malice, and with rapine sweet bereaved
His fierceness of the fierce intent it brought.
That space the Evil One abstracted stood
From his own evil, and for the time remained
Stupidly good, of enmity disarmed,
Of guile, of hate, of envy, of revenge.
But the hot hell that always in him burns,
Though in mid Heaven, soon ended his delight,
And tortures him now more the more he sees
Of pleasure not for him ordained: then soon
Fierce hate he recollects, and all his thoughts
Of mischief, gratulating, thus excites
 – John Milton, *Paradise Lost*

He is my household's guardian soul
He judges, he presides, inspires
All matters in his royal realm...
The fire of his opal eyes,
Clear beacons glowing, living jewels
Taking my measure, steadily
– Baudelaire, *The Cat*

The flat is warm and its windows fogged. It smells of cigarettes, hash, roasting turkey, and clementines. Four stuffed chairs and a two-seat sofa crowd the sitting room. They are draped with throws and fattened out with cushions. Framed and unframed pictures cover the walls – charcoals, oils, gouaches, lithographs, sketches of whom I presume to be family and friends, and souvenir postcards of everyone from Longhi and Moser to Grimshaw. The room was once two rooms but was knocked through, and last night was cleared of the bicycle, laundry, post, and recycling that are ordinarily here. All of the books and vinyl records have been tidied away. Near the French doors to the yard at the back is a table laid for a meal, and crowded by seven mismatched chairs. Everything here is like that: clothes, furniture, cutlery, crockery, records and books are dog-eared, dusty or rusty or scuffed. But it is cosy – made cosier still by the dark, red-painted walls, the coal fire in the grate, fairy lights, and the six foot bough of long-needled pine affixed to the ceiling where a wall once separated the rooms. Homemade paper snowflakes and chocolate coins dangle from the bough. They tantalise me. Everything here might be old and worn, but it's new to me. I only arrived three days ago and already it's Christmas, so it's been a lot to take in.

Of course I sniffed around. The flat is Belinda Bell's. Belinda is slender and small, with hazel eyes and a strong jaw. Her flat is shaped like a squared lowercase letter 'd', lying flat on its back. The bedroom and box room, from where Belinda runs her eBay shop, are adjacent to each other upstairs, on the first floor, as is the bathroom, an extension at the back of the house that forms the stem of the letter 'd'. The kitchen is directly below the bathroom. It is narrow and has an acorn-brown lino floor, a brown-spattered, old gas cooker below a window looking onto the little yard in the back and cabinets you could hide inside. When the half-size refrigerator clicks on it vibrates in e-flat and the magnets on its face describe patterns as erratic as butterfly paths. Belinda has been in the kitchen since sunrise. Chopping and boiling and stuffing and seasoning and basting. Just before guests began to arrive at three she raced upstairs to change for dinner. She is wearing a green, velvet, ankle-length dress with seven buttons on each sleeve, and a high, lace-crested collar. Her hair is swooped up in an onion-shaped pompadour that shows off a grey streak at the front. The grey streak is the first thing you notice (she is only thirty-eight), otherwise her hair is the hue of a dirty copper coin. It's getting on my wick that she's introducing me as Jarvis instead of Geoffrey Cantor (always the full four syllables, thank you very much) as I've been called all of my life. Next person who comes to the door and I'm gone. I don't want to be here when everyone twigs that Lucy isn't coming, when they realise she's disappeared.

Lucy... *oh, Lucy*. You were built for the stage, for the opera, a Wagnerian soprano, with your big hips and chest, your tragic eyes, wide face, wide mouth and big arms – arms that seemed to pull at the air. We never met. But I know about you through The Glaring. I know where you lived and that you ran The Bitch and that you cycled everywhere, even in the rain, and fed the neighbourhood cats who came to your rooftop window. I know that you never asked for help but always offered it. I know you were a virgin, and I know the day you met Him. Belinda was there too. But to her He was just some old man.

It was late afternoon, the 1st of December. Belinda was rolling a cigarette in front of the Dorset. You were trudging up North Street with six shopping bags, rather resembling a powerlifter in the early stages of the clean and jerk. In one bag was a pair of ankle boots from Oxfam and three pairs of woollen knee socks. In another was your horde from the Saturday Market: a pewter letter opener (Secessionist, you thought), a rosewood box probably once used for pens or pins but now good for catnip or weed, a metre of Victorian lace and thirty-six un-inflated balloons. In the three cloth bags were your groceries, a bottle of disinfectant, kitchen roll, and a large scouring sponge. The air was icy. Christmas lights, hung earlier that week, twinkled and blinked. It was one of those wintry afternoons that feels like it belongs to an old photograph or film. The sky was dark; the snow was white. It didn't feel like Brighton but somewhere belonging to the cold, somewhere borne up from the past. A city like Budapest or Prague, with its understorey of secret police and vanished faces. You smiled at how your breath fell before rising and disappearing against the cold, hard darkness of the sky. Then, catching sight of the gulls circling in the high distance, you crunched hurriedly across the street in little Geisha steps. You would have kept going but you spotted a five-pound note, damp and partially obscured by the snow in front of the Dorset. You picked it up.

'Your round then,' Belinda said, simultaneously lighting her roll-up and, reaching behind her, whacking on the electric heater above her head. She was seated at a small, zinc-topped table near the door. There were two dozen or more people huddled in small bundles or at the other tables in front of the pub, and many more passers-by. You laughed and kissed Belinda on each cheek. Then you welled up. You tried covering your eyes but the bags were too heavy for you to lift your hands to your face. Dropping down in the chair opposite Belinda, you stared upward, trying to suck in the tears. Crying embarrassed you. It wasn't your way.

Belinda slitted her eyes. 'Either you've been fucked or you're in love.' She ashed and dragged meditatively. 'If you've been fucked, it wasn't by me, so I don't want to know. But if you're prepared to admit that you're in love with me...' She blew a smoke ring and rhythmically pushed her finger in and out through it. 'Then, my darling, we can talk.'

You laughed again; the relief of it dried your eyes. You hadn't kissed anyone for four years, since you were twenty-eight, other than the night three years ago when you met, and snogged, Belinda. She was working on the coat check at the Hanbury. You were drunk and had lost the ticket for your coat. When you tried to collect it, Belinda flirted with you (later she confessed because she knew you were straight and wanted to see how far she could go). You flirted back (you thought why not). A bargain was reached. You kissed over the countertop. Belinda held your face and you held hers. Someone cheered. You got your coat – and an instant friend. Belinda was one of your closest. You knew that; you know all of this. But you don't know that she almost saved you. You should know that too, in case, like Persephone or the hiccups, you come back.

One of the barmen came and took your order. He had chunky glasses and a glistening quiff. You asked for a mulled cider. Belinda ordered a large glass of red and batted her eyes. The barman pretended to not notice and turned away. Archie, the Dorset's tabby, hopped down from a barrel by the door and inspected the shopping bags at your feet, poking his head in each. You toed the one with the rosewood box out of sight and under your chair. The box was your Christmas present to Belinda. It delighted you to think of the double-entendres she'd make when she opened it. You had a few planned yourself. Archie leapt onto your table and lay on his side beneath the heat lamp. You stroked him. He closed his eyes and rotated his ears to the forward all-listening position. You told Belinda about the gull.

'The Bitch was *such* a bitch yesterday. Black out, no heat. Sorry, I won't go into it.' You held up your hands as though delivering a benediction, or surrendering. 'Went straight to bed when I came home. Friday night, half-seven: rock n' roll. I was just drifting off when I heard something at the bedroom skylight. My first thought – honestly – was that Flip had grown wings. You know Flip – lives two doors down along the roofs, grey with a white belly and green eyes. But I must've been really out of it because it's not a cat up there, but this giant *gull* settled on the roof above the window. You could see its head and neck. I got the feeling he was spying on me, so I watched him back for a few moments, expecting him to screech or fly away. But all he did was turn his head sideways and stare at me. Yellow eyes, like a snake.'

You turn your profile to Belinda, cock your head and open one eye wide. Belinda mirrors you.

'…And stare. And stare. And stare. Then it swings its head to face me and taps its beak on the window – tap, tap – turns and stares at me again. I rolled over on my side. The gull taps the window again, only harder now – *whack*. I ignore him. So – *whack, whack*. I wave my arm at him and peep up. He's staring at me again. So I stare back, sideways, like I'm a gull too.'

You mimic the bird again. Belinda doesn't this time.

'It's a standoff. All I really want is sleep, but I drag myself upright with the duvet over me, like this, and make to open the window to shoo him away. He flies off. I lie down and – tap, tap – stare. I make to open the window again and he flies off like before. But now I'm awake, and have to go to the loo. There's a skylight there too, of course. It's completely daft, but I'm dead on my feet and I think he must know where I've gone and followed me over the roof. I switch off the light and watch the skylight for his head to slide into view. Way, way up there's a flock of gulls circling and gliding. I watch them for a minute or two, to see if I can see what's going on.'

The drinks arrive. You wrap both hands around the glass, inhale the cinnamon and clove-scented steam, and close your eyes. Archie opens his. Belinda scratches under his chin. You touch glasses, and drink.

'Everything looks normal, so I go back to bed. But first I sneak up to the window to check if he's there. Nada. I get under the duvet, snuggle up and – tap, tap – stare. Can you believe it? I mean, he's fucking with me, a bloody *seagull*. I pretend to ignore him. Tap, tap. Tap, tap, tap. Tap, tap – I jump up and bang the window with my fist. But this time he doesn't fly off. He *leaps* on the window, unfurls his wings out to here, *rears* his head back and swings down at me and up and down and up and down like a piston. *Whack, whack, whack, whack, whack, whack* – until – crack! His beak splits. Bits go splintering off. But still he's at it, faster now. *Whackwhackwhackwhackwhackwhack* – right down at me. Then the rest of his beak goes with this incredible snap. He falls so that his eye is like *this, blinking* at me through the window. I threw up everywhere.'

Later you think the drink must have gone to your head – the drink and the roll-up Belinda gave you when you finished telling her about the gull. After that, you could only remember things to a point. You remember Belinda scanning the sky for gulls, giving them the V's and shouting, 'You lot *fuck* off!' You remember it starting to snow, and Belinda's jolt of inspiration to do Christmas at hers. (Were you free? Yes, but you had to work until three or four, and would come after that.) You remember Archie suddenly jerking upright, curling low off the table and hurrying indoors. You had the feeling you were being watched, and kept looking over your shoulder. You told yourself it was only the gull still spooking you. (You didn't buy it, not entirely, but told yourself you did.) You remember Belinda saying, 'One of yours?' and, following her eyes, turning in your chair and seeing Him just as He began singing. Every time you tried to think what happened next, you felt ill.

Let me say it plainly: what happened next happens every day near the corner of Gardner Street and North Road. Someone came and performed. But what happened next doesn't happen every day: everyone turned their heads to watch, and everyone put money in his hat. You were one of those people. You could smell Him from where you were seated fifteen feet away (and He was still in your nose when you returned home). The Old Man smelled like a damp church basement or a dumpster (or the graveyard, from where his clothes came). Soiled white herringbone shirt. Scuffed black boots with flapping outsoles. One orange sock, one yellow, a greasy red cravat. Coal-dark tweed jacket. Flared, blue nylon tracksuit bottoms that fell high above his ankles. His horsehair top hat, now upturned on the ground at His feet, had left a rigid indentation across His brow. His head was enormous.

Some people swear that the Old Man was tall – taller than the five-foot-ten He actually was. He had a long neck and His fingers were spidery. But then others are adamant He was short. He was age-stooped and between His shoulder blades His back showed signs of a hump. His broken halo of red-grey hair caught the wind like a wild semaphore, and His arms hung forward, insect like, when He sang. No one noticed Him when He shuffled up; He was just another beggar or busker; and it was too snowy, too cold to pay Him any attention. But when He started to sing a strange warmth moved through the crowd, a warmth like a voluptuous Yes. Like a living being that could kick its heels in the air, buy a round, kiss, cop a feel, tremble, laugh, weep, and screw. The Old Man began with *O Isis und Osiris*; your fingers found the fiver in your coat pocket. It was everything you had on you and you knew then that you would give Him everything.

The song bled into the next. You were momentarily lost, your heart adding an extra beat, an indignant counter-thump when the Old Man sang: '*If you should ever leave me...*' Gooseflesh ran up your arms and neck. You leapt to your feet, swallowing hard to *Man of Constant Sorrow*. The next song was too much: *Winner Takes it All*: you rushed forward, holding forth the fiver as though it was a fishing rod. You stopped short, you continued nervously, tentatively, hoping at once that the Old Man would acknowledge you (a knowing wink, a raised palm, a tusky grin) or blank you. Grit crunched under your feet. You threw your money in His hat and everything went white. It was the same for everyone. They stopped drinking, shopping, toasting, talking, driving, moaning and emptied their pockets and purses and wallets into His top hat. Twenty pound notes, tenners, coins by the fistful...

Some time later you were home and standing at your sitting room window watching the blizzard blanket Seven Dials. Fiona, Flip's sister and frequent antagonist, sharpened her claws on the back of your sofa, then hopped up and crouched on its armrest. It was night. Your face was puffy and red, the cuffs of your jumper damp with snot and tears. But you don't remember any of it any more than you remember returning home. Every time you thought about Him the room started to spin. In other words, Belinda had been prophetic on two counts: you were in love and you were fucked.

I want to shake you. If I could, I would have taken you by the arms and shaken you. Look at Him, Lucy. Look at that beautiful youth you see, that outsized urchin, and see the Old Man with His scored and ashen skin, see His cracked and fallen face. Don't you see? Don't you see? Look out for Him. Listen for Him: His caramelised voice with a touch of scratch, His bunion-toed footfalls that clop like the hooves of a goat.

The next day was dark and there was more snow. Trains froze on the tracks and there were few cars on the streets. The sea was quiet and low, as though cowering in anticipation of a beating. There was no sun, and day became night and in the night the haar – that curious, velvety sea fog – swallowed everything in its briny eddies.

At 7 o'clock the following morning, Lucy arrived at work to supervise the volunteers who came to prepare – and to eat – the free vegan breakfast The Bitch provided three times weekly to Brighton's homeless and unemployed. Everyone called it The Bitch because of its acronym, BHITC, a shortening of Brighton & Hove Intercommunity Therapeutic Centre. Lucy ran The Bitch. She had started eight years earlier as a volunteer, teaching an intermediate IT workshop and working on a rough sleepers outreach team. Not long afterward, she was asked to run The Bitch's fundraising appeal for a new community kitchen. When a year later the Managing Director, Harriet Potts, a curly-mulleted old bean with a taste for merlot and stern women, had a nervous breakdown, Lucy was the only candidate on the shortlist to replace her. She threw herself into it. Until the recession came, The Bitch achieved three consecutive year-end break-even bank balances, and one year a modest surplus, its first for a decade. Day and evening classes expanded to include qigong, advanced Photoshop, a mindfulness and authentic movement masterclass and Japanese calligraphy. A new, four console IT suite in the corner of the cafeteria was installed and earned The Bitch as much as sixty or seventy pounds a day. Staff and volunteers nicknamed Lucy 'The Queen'. Privately, Lucy worried that this meant Queen Bitch, and consequently wasn't as authoritative as she ought to have been. Instead of assigning or delegating work, she did it herself. Lucy worked twelve or fourteen hour days three or four days a week, and often stopped by work on weekends to finish a funding application, to deliver a digital media workshop when an instructor was ill, or to lend a hand with the family gardening project. She told herself that if BHITC could be called The Bitch, then it would LAC nothing, so long as she, Lucy Ann Cuthman, had a say. It was a poor and conceited pun that she never said aloud to anyone but herself at home on those days when she needed to overcome the urge to jack it in and go backpacking across Thailand for as long as she could afford.

Lucy was 'Lucy' because of the Beatles song, from the first album her father had ever purchased with his own money. Ann had been her grandmother's name on her mother's side. The Cuthmans could trace their roots back to Devon before the Norman Conquest, to Saxon times, and specifically to a gaunt and umbriferous-bearded shepherd who, with little more than his bare hands and the strength afforded him by his belief in the Almighty, built a church on the bank of the River Adur, and preached himself into sainthood.

Aside from spiritual devotion, Lucy was every bit his descendent in tenacity as much as name. And aside from a tearful trimester boarding at a Warwickshire girls school (her mother was ill and her father had passed away), Lucy had always lived near the sea. Seven years in Falmouth, five each in Exmouth and Bristol, four in Aberdeen, seven months handing out nightclub flyers in Lisbon, six months on Sark, and a summer in Crete, where her skin went sugary-brown and her hair bleached platinum-white. (Until she had been running The Bitch for a year, Lucy's mass of matted, dark-blonde hair was plaited with green, purple and red threads. Her hair was still long today, a voluminous tangle of consonants and vowels, of S's, and J's and C's, of O's and U's). Arriving in Brighton, she had squatted in Powys Square and Denmark Terrace before letting and then buying a slope-ceilinged, one bedroom flat with two skylights, three storeys above a DIY shop on Seven Dials. Its sitting room and bedroom were at either end of the flat and a short hallway ran between. The hallway wallpaper was a pattern of thousands of tiny oxeye daisies – an at once soothing and dizzying pattern Lucy had chosen as a housewarming present to herself. There were shiny streaks on it from where she would trail her fingers over the flowers on her way to bed or out the door and around the light switch casing. From home it was a twelve minute cycle to work. Uphill, downhill, past the Pavilion, then uphill again.

But because of the snow and the haar that Monday, Lucy had been forced to walk. It was dark when she left her flat around half-six that morning. There were no buses. The snow was several inches deep and she walked in the street. Alongside the Church of St Nicholas, she followed a trail of paw prints until a gust of wind lifted her hat from her head and sent it tumbling along the road. Lucy chased it down and when she had shoved it back on, something nearby seemed to moan the word *Home*. *Home*: it sounded six or seven times. Lucy turned in a circle to see who – or what – it was. But there was no one there. The sound vanished in the wind and a chill shook her. Her toes and fingertips tingled and her face was burned rosy red by the time she arrived at work.

Nearly half an hour passed before a full crew of kitchen volunteers arrived and it was another thirty minutes after that that breakfast was ready and the cafeteria was decently warmed. The Bitch was housed in a red-brick Victorian schoolhouse in Hadley Place, a rectangular cul-de-sac off Kingswood Hill, in Kemp Town. A canvas banner strung between the first floor windows above the front door announced its full, elongated name in bright, hand-painted, primary colours. Reception, adult education classrooms and children's activity rooms were on the ground floor and the community kitchen, community laundry, cafeteria, and crèche were on the second. In between was a warren of hallways and offices either side of a stairwell. Every office gave way onto one or two other offices that were either larger or smaller (never the same) than the one that preceded it, or narrow hallways that, as frequently as not, meant a step or two up or down, depending on which way you were travelling. The effect was Escher-like.

Lucy took a bowl of porridge and a cup of tea to her office. There were two routes to it, and two doors. The 'front' door (to which her desk was set at a right angle, like her teachers' classroom desks so frequently had been) opened onto Judith and Michaela's office, that itself could only be reached after first passing through Lauren's. Before Lauren's there was a short hallway narrowed in half by a bank of filing cabinets and, beyond that, the stairwell that smelled perennially of lentils and nuns: of the present and the past. Running behind all three offices was a striplight lit corridor with six doors: three opened onto the 'back' of the offices on Lucy's side of the passage, the other three onto the dissembled Russian doll of interconnected rooms across the way.

Rather than breakfasting at her desk, Lucy switched on the

Dimplex heater near the front windows and perched on a chair beside it. The windows were ferned with frost; outside the haar hid from view the cul-de-sac below, over which The Bitch scowled like a widowed and embittered marchioness. Hadley Place was bound on the left by the dark brick spine of terraced houses on the parallel street and to the right by a sharply sloping bramble-tangled lot behind a chain-link fence. Straight ahead, on the far side of Kingswood Hill, was a four-storey car park with a concrete façade that wept rustily year round. Beyond that was the university, the bustling clubs and cafés of St James' Street, the meringue-like seafront houses and be-flagged B&Bs that on clear days gazed out onto The Channel and that morning saw nothing beyond the wall of fog that formed an icy cataract between the land and the sky and wheezing sea.

Lucy's morning was phone calls and emails: the auditors, the bank, the solicitors, the city council, the plasterers who had two weeks earlier started on the ground floor loos and then not shown again, social services, the police, the job centre and the family support unit at the wet hostel in Portslade. Lunch was a cup of instant miso soup, two bananas and a dozen more emails. Then it was a management review of The Bitch's health and safety policy, its volunteer recruitment policy, its safeguarding procedure and the budget. Lucy drank three coffees. She had a 90-minute conference call with her chairman and the head of a PR agency. Darkness fell. Lucy spent two hours drafting another grant application to keep The Bitch's homeless employment training project running. Without one hundred and twelve thousand pounds the project would close before the New Year had little more than a moment to stretch its legs. Close and sixty or seventy unemployed and homeless men and women who didn't want to be homeless and unemployed, who hated being homeless and unemployed, who were ashamed of it and wanted to work, wanted somewhere permanent to live (and wanted to be able to look people in the eye again, wanted to be able to look their children in the eyes) would stay homeless and unemployed. Close and Lucy would need to make staff unemployed. Unemployed, they risked homelessness. Homeless, they would be back at The Bitch for free vegan breakfasts three days a week. Today's grant application – and there had been fourteen others submitted in the weeks before it – was due in two days, at noon. Lucy wrote hard and almost without interruption until six o'clock, when Meg, who volunteered at reception, came to say goodnight. Judith and Michaela left with her. Amy, Lauren, Ada, Susie, and David could be heard as they passed through the front door. Weather had forced the cancellation of tonight's English as a Second Language class, and the beginners' belly dancing had broken early for Christmas. In the stillness, Lucy listened to the rubbery hiss of the front door easing itself shut again and again as the rest of the staff and volunteers and visitors left for the night, the loud clack of the lock snapping into place. Everyone gone, Lucy sat quietly at her desk for half an hour, anonymously surfing dating websites and news channels before a final look at her emails. There were another twenty since she had last checked. None were from donors (where *would* that £112,000 come from)? But one was from Wiggy, with CLIT? as its subject line.

CLIT...? CLIT...? Lucy thrummed her fingers on her bottom lip. In their game, Lucy, Wiggy, Belinda, Edward, Bodhi, Anna, and Alan (and anyone else with the puerility to play) used acronymical charity-speak to come up with new projects for The Bitch. There were two ways to play. Present the acronym as a challenge to the others to fill in the blanks, or spell it out in all its words for everyone else to dissemble into the acronym. The more right-on or worthier the programme sounded, the better. It had begun when Lucy failed to dissuade a new committee at The Bitch from naming itself Volunteer Action Group. Eventually, the group had disbanded – or as Lucy (wearing her best Easter Island expression) announced to Wiggy and a few others over a drink, had dried up. But CLIT…? CLIT…?

Lucy had teased out *Cultural Learning Insight Team* when she noticed the time in the corner of her computer screen was 19:19. It was the third time that day she'd seen this sort of harmony or doubling. At the afternoon management meeting she had spilt coffee on her mobile and, blotting it dry, had seen the time was 14:14. At 17:17 she had briefly stopped working on the grant application to cross the room and peer through the fog at the snowball fight below her window. Now here it was again. The first two instances occurred three hours apart, and there were two hours between the second and the third, as though time was shortening, or as though something was drawing itself closer upon her.

What I know about Him I know from the few days we lived together – an icy three weeks that began in the dark, early hours of December, the same night that the gull, pyretic and brainless with lunacy, hammered itself to death trying to get at Lucy as she lay alone in bed – and through what passed through The Glaring, the ever-watchful, purling and quietly garrulous clan (grouped, somewhat still, by a centuries-old districting) of which I am a member by birthright. There were seventy-eight of us locally, and hundreds more throughout the postcode, the eyes and spies of the city, steadily measuring, steadily observing and recording all there was to hear, sense and see from gardens, rooftops, windows, the twittens and streets. From pubs, homes, cafés and eavesdropped tête-à-têtes on the telephone, nothing bent from our lithe and proprietary ear. Aside from keeping our own hours, a tendency toward taciturnity and, rather conversely, a predisposition to conversation, as housemates the Old Man and I had little in common. Take for instance the bathroom incident a day or two after He had moved Himself in without a word and with no more than He wore on His self and in His dark, vulpine eyes. Upon encountering it, 'Christ,' I said to myself, blinking. 'Will you look at that.' There, bobbing on the surface of the all but frozen toilet bowl water, was a heart-shaped shit.

The Old Man had been in here before me, I knew: the hircine scrabble up the stairs; the creak of the floorboards; the renowned pause... and then the same sounds in lackadaisical reverse. But because I'd never known Him to actually use the loo – there was no toilet roll, and despite the constant rivulet down the back of the bowl, when it came to flushing, there was no missing it – the whole house seemed to groan and shiver – after He'd gone I hurried in. I was parched and, in all of the house, the first floor loo water was the most refreshing. And now this: a heart-shaped shit, roughly the size of a beefed-up garden snail, and as dark as a crow. The smell, now that it had warmed in my nostrils, was pure... And was it bobbing so much as actually *beating*?

No, this wasn't on. No. It's not like *I* go around leaving *my* turds about for anyone to inspect. There are principles for these things. There is decorum. No: I left the loo thirstily and, next I saw Him, I had words. Not that I think He paid me any mind.

We lived at 9 Clifton Gardens, a mid-terrace, white-stuccoed house, a fifteen minute uphill amble from the sea. It smelled of books: there were once over three thousand, and they had been in every room. From the front bay windows there was, in order of propinquity, a tidy, south-facing garden (hollyhocks, alum, bay tree, lavender, birdsong that made your heart race), the vaulted pavement, the road, a gated, semi-public garden with tumbling rhododendron and a quarter acre of lawn that ran the length of the street, a hillside of houses and shops sloping down toward The Lanes and, beyond that, the pebble beach and pewter-green sea. The garden at the back of the house was all ferns, potted herbs and crazy paving, with cat grass and Irish moss growing in between. There was a wrought-iron table for four and, at the very back, about thirty feet from the house, a high, knobbly flint wall with a door in its centre that led to the twitten – the narrow and ever shadowed passage or alleyway –

that ran behind all of the houses on Clifton Gardens, from Dyke Road to Montpelier Rise. Built in 1847 (there was a crest above the front door) the house had been home to the Sindens, the Pococks, the Knights, the Howells, the Boswells (yes: relatives of), the Woods, the Shaws, the Garners, the Gardners, the Tugwells, a man called Pugh, a woman named Tabitha Inch (a fin de siècle police constable) and a family of Halls. Among the inhabitants had been a playwright, three school teachers, a wine cellerman, a tailor, two opium eaters, a needlewoman, a grocer, a painter, a preacher, an infantryman who never returned from the Somme, three charwomen, a retired mariner, and the two musicians, Ernie and Margaret Rothenberg, whom I lived with until they died. He taught at the university and she saw students at home. Together, the Rothenbergs played the accordion, the oud, zither, violin, and guitar. Ernie played the cello and cornet, and Margaret the flute, bassoon and trombone. Both of them sang and accompanied the other on the piano. There was music every day.

Margaret died first, a year and some before Ernie. Angina: she was seventy-eight. After she went, there was no more music at home. The house was as tidy as ever, but the music was gone. And Ernie began wearing Margaret's underwear. Through his clothes you could make out the bra straps over his shoulders, the flattened bra cups bunched on his chest, the ring of her girdle over his belly. Her laddered stockings showed above his socks when he crossed his legs and his trousers rode up his shins. It was his way of keeping her close. But there was no more music. He missed her; it's what killed him. One wet April morning (when the waxflower and phlox in the front garden were beginning to bloom) he didn't wake up. Ernie died wearing Margaret's nightdress and, in that way, I like to think he didn't die alone.

I hid when they came to take his body away. I hid and – eyes closed, ears alert and twitching – listened to them talk about probate and intestacy. There were no next of kin; I knew I'd get nothing. And I was still hiding when they locked up the house. Front door, cat flap, garden door, anti-squatting steel shutters over the windows: the works. But it didn't stop the squatters. They came that same night. The cat flap was in the utility room at the back of the house, set in the window above the washing machine. I watched from the night shadows as the squatters wrenched off the steel shutter over the utility room window, punched open the flap, stretched an arm in and, after much straining and grunting, undid the window latch. The first slipped in through the window; the rest came through the back door. Two, then three, then two more. I ran away. But a day later I came home; there was nowhere else to go. The squatters let me stay. For a year and a half, I dossed in whichever room they weren't using. Then the Old Man moved in, a few hours before the first December dawn, and overnight they were gone. The house took on a different timbre. The windows shook and it whistled hollow and low in the cold sea wind.

I should have been there at the end, not Lucy. It was my home. I am old and worthless.

No one can tell you why, at 19:19 and alone at The Bitch, Lucy didn't run in the opposite direction when she heard the strange footfalls in the rear passageway. They came at alternating gaits, as though their owner (for what can we own, if not our walk) was shifting between a shuffle, then a drag or slither and then a hurried and nimble clippity-clop, clippity-clop, until they seemed to stop outside her door.

Lucy watched for the handle to turn. She called hello. No one answered; the handle stayed as it was. From time to time in the past, a homeless client or another would sequester themselves in some quiet corner of the building, only to awaken or emerge once everyone had gone for the night. Food and equipment had gone missing. Lucy had had locks installed on every door; now even the toilets were to be locked at night. After another few moments passed, she decided whoever it was must have entered one of the rooms across the corridor.

She looked. The corridor was dark. It smelled of winter and dust. A light shone in the stairwell at the far end. Lucy blinked until her eyes adjusted to the low light. There was no one there. A flake of plaster fell from the ceiling, swaying slowly back and forth like a feather as it dropped. Lucy began trying the doors. The other two on her side of the corridor were locked, as were the first two she tried across the way. But the third was not, and because the three offices were interconnected, Lucy doubled back through the first two to see who was there. She switched on the overhead light in each room and looked behind the desks, the cabinets and chairs. She stood still for a moment, listening for breathing, listening to the silence. She was certain she had heard someone before. Now she would have to check every door in the building.

The chill was stronger in the stairwell, a damp, clinging chill. Lucy rubbed her hands to warm them between checking the doors to the café, the kitchen, the crèche, the laundry, the woodworking shop, the toilets on the second floor, on the ground floor and the five adult education and children's activity rooms. All were locked and there was no sound other than the brisk, papery noise Lucy made rubbing her hands together, and the peel of her footsteps where the floor was sticky from spilt tea and the creosote that had seeped to the surface of the old wooden boards.

The building's front door was directly below Lucy's office. To make certain it was locked, she opened it and, leaning backwards, used both hands to heave it closed against the air brakes. The lock clacked loudly back into place. A puff of icy fog that had slipped in swirled about Lucy and then scattered, as though suddenly summoned elsewhere. Lucy made her way back up the stairwell, through Lauren's, then Judith's and Michaela's unlit offices – until, nearing her own, she felt her nape go tight. From somewhere in the dark had come the sound of phlegmy crepitation. Lucy froze and listened for it again. At first there was nothing. But then she heard it from some distance behind her, from where she had just been. Then it was closer, it was in the room with her. Then it came from the other side of her partly open office door. Lucy took a step backward, and stretched out her hands behind her in the dark. She stopped, and there was silence. She breathed out. The sound came again, once more from her office. Lucy slowly crept to her door and very slowly pushed it open.

The room was in a grey and crepuscular half-light, lit only by the fog-shrouded front door lantern below Lucy's office windows and, some ten or twelve feet away, the little Anglepoise lamp on her desk. The Old Man stood in profile near the centre of the floor. His top hat was on His head, and His body twitched like a dog's fur leaps from fleas. Teeth bared, He stared in wide horror at some point on the ceiling. His long and soiled fingers were splayed rigidly at His sides.

Your heart raced at the beautiful boy of twenty-six here again before you, rosy-cheeked from the outdoors, eyes downcast to have to come to you for help, and shivering from the cold. He was dressed in the same ragged castoffs he had been wearing when you first saw him two days earlier. Evidently, they were his only clothes. 'You were... Saturday... at the Dorset... you sing so...' you managed. Then in a burst, 'If you need housing or something to eat or if I can —'

'Thou wert,' said the Old Man through His teeth, burnishing each word with disgust, 'Five. Pound. Note.' With His pinkie, He went to work at and withdrew something from inside His ear. He held it up to His eyes then sniffed it. Caught on the underside of His nail was a moist yellow-brown scoop of wax; there was more on the top. Rolling all of it into a ball between His fingers, He dropped it into His breast pocket. Then, all at once, He removed

His top hat, reached inside it and withdrew a stiff five pound note that He began to wave forward and back and forward and back, slowly at first, then faster and faster, until the paper made a snapping noise, and He slapped it down onto the desk.

Your blush spread across your chest and burnt your face when the boy said he remembered seeing you outside the Dorset. He confessed he was only able to steal a glance then – and again now, his eyes seemed to add, as he removed his top hat and daubed at his forehead with a handkerchief, then quickly thrust it to his mouth as a wracking cough shook him, and he was forced to brace himself on your desk. You saw him peep at you as though to make certain you were watching and then, with a discreet flourish, tuck his handkerchief into his jacket pocket. You resisted the urge to test his brow for fever. Test it, you saw, and what was to stop you from soothing it with a kiss? And if you kissed his forehead, what would stop you from…You grabbed the doorknob to anchor yourself across the room.

Turning toward Lucy His fixed and horrified stare, He saw in her unbearable virtue and beauty, saw in her an awful readiness to help Him, saw that it was everything she could do not to rush forward and hold Him in her arms, and saw in Himself unbuttoned vileness and mourned all that He was and had lost. His face was folklorically wrinkled and grey and patches of stubble grew thick and black from the moles surrounding His mouth, forever twisted agape, as though set in a permanent howl. His eyes were dark and the lids frostbitten and red raw. One of His ears was set higher than the other and was pointed at the back, as if He had been hooked by some unseen fisherman high above. His breath was bellicose. It was weaponised.

A sensation of everything-has-come-to-this awakened inside you. You saw in the boy a bashful and epicene beauty, saw in him vulnerability, an artist unarmoured. Saw hunger, saw fever and wounded pride; saw him in your arms, and you in his. The boy's lips were moist and full, his eyes brown and sorrowful (he was

20

hungry, you could see – very hungry and very cold), and his neck delicate. He had a narrow and feminine jaw. The collar of his shirt was absently askew, flipped upright on one side where the other lay flat beneath his threadbare jacket. The smell of wood smoke clung to his tousled poet's hair. You thought of Rossetti, when he was young. And him in your arms and you in his. Seasons passed.

'I'm Lucy,' you started, intending to say more, but a shiver seized the boy, then a coughing fit that shook him harder than before. You hurried toward him, but he waved you back. The coughing crescendoed and subsided. The boy laughed quickly, barely more than a sputter, as though in disbelief at the pitifulness of his condition. You asked him if he'd like a cup of tea. Nodding yes, he rested his top hat on your desk and said, 'Two sugars, please.'

The electric kettle was atop a filing cabinet in Lauren's office, next door but one. Teabags and sugar were in bowls beside the kettle. Bottles of tap water and milk were on the windowsill. At this time of year, miniature shards of ice would form in the milk and the top quarter inch of water would solidify in a frozen disc overnight.

The kettle began to whir. You rooted through the filing cabinet for biscuits, shaking your head and having a whispered word with yourself. *Stop acting so… You're in charge here. Get a… Do your job. You* know *this. Check the Belltower Hostel, St Patrick's, the Nightstop in Hove…Greta might even have a room at…* Two sugars?

'Was it two sugars, or one? Or none?' you called through the doorway, pleased, now, with the calmness of your voice. Lauren's office was lit, but, between it and yours, Michaela's and Judith's was dark. You waited a moment for the boy to reply. You called out again. Nothing. The kettle whirred louder. You started across the darkened room, worried that the boy – so sickly, so weak, so beautiful – had passed out, hit his head, and scolded yourself for not having taken him straight to hospital. He was frail, he needed help; and you'd failed him. You called hello, wincing at the desperation re-entering your voice. The kettle boiled louder and clicked off when you reached your office. It was empty. You checked behind the desk, then flung open the back door when, through the window, came the hiss of the front door below, easing itself shut with a loud clack.

Twirling on your coat and scarf, you only half-registered the time in the corner of your computer screen – not until later did you tell yourself that it couldn't have possibly been right: 19:19. And in your haste to go after the boy, you missed the newspaper-wrapped bundle on your desk where he had lain his top hat.

How the Old Man shrieked when you told Him your name. Lucy, how He screamed.

Christmas morning I woke around five and nosed about for something to eat. There were a few biscuits on a plate in the kitchen. I ate them quickly, got sick and went back to sleep hungry. When Belinda woke a couple of hours later we had a proper breakfast: soft boiled eggs with soldiers and pâté. Belinda insisted on cutting everything into little chunks. It got my back up, but I blinked thanks just the same, scoffed the lot, then dozed while she wrapped presents, including one for me, and got down to work in the kitchen.

Sabrina came to me in my dream. Sabrina had lived in luxury around the corner from Clifton Gardens, in a balconied, sixteen-windowed Powis Place villa with an hourglass-shaped rear garden filled with fruit trees, sunlight, topiaried hedges and a deep emerald lawn. Sabrina and I... We would lie together all afternoon, hardly moving, stretched out on our backs, feeling the sun warm us right through. Other times, when it was cold, we would curl up; never have two lovers slept together so beauti-fully. People talk about spoons and spooning; we were like a collision, all arms and legs and backbones and bellies and tongues and soft sounds, like the sea being sucked slowly back through the pebbles into itself once again. My dream of Sabrina was fantasy. In it, she didn't die. She had gone on holiday to the south of France instead. Always so irreverent about things like *fate* and *destiny* and *death,* she kept moving from seat to footwell to seat all over the car (what seatbelt could ever hold her) and was jettisoned through an open window when they piled into the backside of a colossal harvesting machine reversing out of a hidden lane. She was found wounded and amnesic by a vinous old farmer who, charitable and eccentric (or just radiantly bonkers), nursed her back to health in some ramshackle barn or outbuilding of his after the local Gendarmerie had investigated, photographed, swept up and hosed down the crash scene. An arduous cross-country journey later, characterised by sudden downpours and stolen food, furtive kips atop hayricks and water gulped straight from streams, brought her to Dieppe, where she stowed away on a night ferry to Newhaven. Then a lift from a camp and kindly lorry driver as far as the clock tower in Brighton city centre and she came bouncing along the sun-dappled street and, like a pair of besotted Eskimos, we touched noses hello like we always did.

A few weeks earlier, before I came to stay with Belinda and was still living in Clifton Gardens, I woke one night to the sound of singing and told myself it must be a dream. My first thought was that, somehow, the Rothenbergs were back. Then I wondered if, in my sleep, I'd gone to wherever they'd gone off to. But when I felt the cold on my toes and saw that I was indeed still in the empty bedroom one floor above the sitting room, where the piano had been, and where Ernie and Margaret, whenever the spirit took them, would entertain themselves or friends, I crept downstairs, sleek as time, to see what was happening, keeping as quiet as I could, lest in my haste I burst or spoil things. It was the voices of two people singing the aria of *Dido's Lament.* They sang in harmony, three octaves apart. The higher voice was feminine, alighting and fluttering with oscine beauty, and the lower voice oozing like a dark wound. But rather than Ernie and Margaret, I found the Old Man, alone. His arms hung strangely from His shoulders and were cocked at the elbow and wrist like a praying mantis. The room was smoky from the lank fire in the fireplace and lit only by the heavy-shaded lamp near the steel-shuttered windows that once overlooked the rear garden.

I listened from the doorway until He had finished. Then I announced myself. A day or two earlier I had confronted the Old Man about the heart-shaped shit. It vanished without a word (or a flush, for that matter). He hadn't spoken to me since.

But now, He almost purred, 'Sir.' And as though He had been holding a lit match all the while, with a wave of His hand a lusty and fizzing fire sprung up in the hearth. My whiskers quickened. I started forward, but stopped. 'Please,' He said with a sweeping gesture. 'Draw thee near the fire, for I observe that despite thy heavy coat thou hast chill in thy old bones.'

He smiled, and I saw that He was missing teeth either side of His left canine (stalactitic and brown) and a third was missing on the other side, at the bottom front. I didn't think much of it, at first. But taking a wide arc toward the fire I, with a swipe of my tongue, quickly checked that all of my own teeth were still there, top and bottom, other than the one had I lost on a Chinese takeaway many years before.

For a long time we both stared into the fire. My mistrust of strangers meant I watched Him from the corner of my eye. I could feel Him doing the same. After a while, I sensed He had turned His full gaze toward me; and if it had not been for the fire, I would have bolted from the room. His eyes were like the thin, dark ice that forms atop puddles in the night: the slightest step and you were straight through, arms windmilling as you plummeted into the oubliette that He was. And I had the impression His face was continuously dissolving and reassembling into new forms. You never saw it when you looked at Him straight on, but only obliquely, from an angle of unease. One moment His nose was where it should be, His nostrils as twiggy and bristling as the limbs of an under-stitched scarecrow; then it seemed to vanish, only to reappear on His jaw to snuffle around His neck and chin. His skin fell away like powder, momentarily reforming in healthy hues of youth, before greying and sagging and creasing. His eyebrows grew long, disappeared and reformed over His lips and then inchwormed up His cheeks into place again.

Yes, I would have run from the room, but the fire seduced me. Its warmth, its dance. I crouched before it.

'*She.*' And He spoke Lucy's name, as though aiming a weapon at himself. 'Who is *she* to remain so content, so driven, so pure? Doth not the seasons change? Doth not pride and ambition serve to tempt, much as the sea strips the shore? They doeth; and the sea shall riseth to swallow this white city, this bright haven. The ground shall fissure, thy homes crack and fall, and the great dark damp rise to swallow it whole. All in this shining recess shall drown. Only *she*, should she consent to be my consort, my clean-holed whore...' And what began as a prim, self-satisfied smile twisted into a grin. It was then that I noticed He was missing two teeth on the bottom left, where before He had been missing none, and that where the two blackened gaps had stood sentry either side of His rotting fang, now were a tooth and a half, now more, as the rest of the half tooth grew into place and gleamed in His jaw.

When I looked again all of His teeth were there and He beamed at me like a weatherman. Then His face swelled red. He gagged and a fly flew out of His mouth. A fly – a bluebottle – at this time of year! I swatted it down and stood on it, feeling its buzz vibrate up my leg, until the buzz fell flat.

We were silent again. After some time had passed I felt His hand on my shoulder.

'I shall tell thee all as it was.' His hand began dropping slowly, slowly down my spine. The Old Man was several paces away, yet I was certain it was His hand on me, as though it had dissolved like His face had done and reappeared on His ankle or, like some awful fruit, fallen from His shin to scuttle on silent fingertips across the floor and find me. I raised my chin. The flames swayed in enchanting rhythm. My eyes grew heavy. His hand dropped lower and lower and, so slowly, lightened in its descent, until it was no longer His hand but two fingers, then one, that, when it reached the base of my spine, swivelled unhurriedly and found its mark. 'And how upon arrival I came. For though I canst see in thy eyes thou knowest thy share of abandonment and suffering, it measures nothing,' the pressure of His finger grew stronger, until I was forced to give way, and it narrowed in, 'to the unenviable throne that stands as horrent and unresting reminder of the state from whence I fell. *I was a star…*'

The concreted area in front of Lucy's building was separated from the pavement and from the front areas of the neighbouring terraced houses by low walls. A wide un-gated opening to one side of the front wall was marked on either side by two squat and white-rendered pillars. On days when the weather was fine, the area served as an extra display case for the DIY shop on the ground floor: galvanised garden incinerators and brooms, bags of coal and sacks of firewood and flowerpots and window boxes, and more. A path from the opening in the wall led to Lucy's front door, which was black-painted, heavy and narrow. At its base was a small black and white-tiled stoop. Spring and autumn the front door swelled from condensation; unlocked it still took a kick to open it. In the winter it could freeze shut and took many kicks. There were forty-four stairs up to Lucy's flat, and around two-thirds of the way up there was a lockable interior door that separated Lucy's rooms from the rest of the building.

Beyond this door (which was flimsy and opened with no

kicking at all) was a small landing, with jackets and cycling gear hanging from coat hooks, umbrellas, wellies, old trainers, and the final fourteen foot-worn stairs up to Lucy's flat. From her sitting room windows, there was a partial view of the green slopes and whaleback swells of the South Downs. The room itself felt like an elevated extension or satellite of the Downs, with its six or seven large potted plants, battered brown sofa, and a rug crocheted to look like grass. The kitchen was merely a segment of the sitting room, separated by a cluttered countertop beneath a coved archway. Lucy kept a pint glass of water and a small plate of dry food on the kitchen floor for the visiting cats who, in their approach to her flat, were not unlike those mountain goats that scale sheer cliff faces to nibble at high altitude nettles or to simply contemplate the busy and embattled world below. The cats posed atop chimney pots, sprang from window ledges and stalked birds, having emerged through cat flaps, open windows and rooftop terrace doors of the neighbouring houses. They came and went through Lucy's bedroom skylight, through which the afternoon sun shone and warmed the bed Lucy had positioned to ensure the pillows remained in the shade and cool. The cats would jump down on to the bed when the skylight was open, or opened for them. From the bedside table they would elongate (as cats do) to catch hold of the window ledge in the sloped ceiling with their out-splayed claws and hoist themselves through and out again.

Far below, set in the wall beside Lucy's front door, was a railing that rose in black enamelled arrowhead spikes. Lucy's bicycle was secured to the railing. Its rear tyre rested on the ground and its front was raised so to reach the iron bars to which it was locked. To Lucy it looked like an excited dog or foal leaping to see her; she wanted to clap for it to make it come and, out of habit, would pat its saddle. When she returned home the night the boy had turned up unannounced at The Bitch, she brushed off the snow. As she did so the bicycle lurched backward, as though rearing away out of fright.

Lucy righted it and, after four kicks, let herself in and wearily climbed the stairs to run a hot bath and, from there, to bed. There was leftover soup in the refrigerator, but her appetite was gone. Just a hot cup of tea, hot bath, hot water bottle and bed. Maybe in her dreams, she said aloud to herself, things would work out. Lucy had chased after the boy, helloing through the haar in Hadley Place and Kingswood Hill, but he had vanished. She had rung The Bitch's outreach team. Nothing: no one matching the boy's description. She checked at the Market Diner, imagining him huddled over a cup of tea, and rang half a dozen hostels to see if he had found a bed with them. She checked at the YMCA on the Old Steine and at the halfway house across from the postal sorting office in North Road. Checked the car park behind the Brighthelm Centre where rough sleepers slept, checked beneath the Community Base canopy and the darkened doorways of the cafés and clothing shops in Queens Road as far down as the clock tower, and then up the other side of the street past the Masonic Centre, and there was nothing and nobody and the boy was nowhere. The wind cracked up and blew white sighs off the rooftops and off the cars imprisoned by snow. When the bells of St Nicholas sounded eleven, Lucy had headed home. Cold had seeped through her boots and her feet were damp and numb.

As she neared her flat, she had tripped over a snowy clump beside the deep, metal dumpster on the street. There had been no rubbish collection that week because of the weather and bags of garbage and household debris were piled up on the kerbside. Lucy went down fast, her fall broken by a rolled up rug that unfurled on impact. She left it there, flat in the street atop the snow.

Home, the sound rose up again in the wind. In the lengthening dark and rising damp it sounded: *Home*.

I should have been there to warn you, Lucy. When you came to

Clifton Gardens, when you came to my home, I should have warned you away. I am plagued by guilt. It ruins me.

* * *

'And here's where we do the lantern-making workshops,' Lucy said holding open the cafeteria door for the PR girl. It was the morning after the boy had shown-up in Lucy's office and she had searched for him in the night. The PR girl was about twenty-four and wore high leather boots, a faux fur headband and a dark blue coat with hidden buttons. The cafeteria smelled of coffee and porridge and toast. Around twenty men and women break-fasted with slow solemnity at the half-dozen large, wooden-topped tables beneath the south- and west-facing walls, which were made entirely of windows, and through which the haar loomed like the eyes of the dead. The lanterns were for the Burning of the Clocks, an annual procession on the night of the winter solstice to mark the year's end. The procession of school-children, parents and dancers snaked and drummed through The Lanes and along the seafront, where a two-storey effigy was lit and collapsed on itself into a bonfire, beneath a firework display that drew twenty thousand or more spectators.

'Workshops are run by volunteers two afternoons and evenings a week, and Saturdays ten till two. The closer we get to the solstice, the busier we are, so with one week to go we're doing workshops every day. It's non-stop.'

'How *int*eresting.'

'We typically get twenty, twenty-five children between five and ten or eleven-years-old, and about as many parents every session. Usually it's just mums, but dads have started coming too. We're even seeing some fourteen and fifteen-year-olds coming on their own now, kids who used to come with their parents and are now bringing their friends. In the beginning, for the first two or three years, we had sixty or so people with lanterns. Last year it was nine hundred.'

'How *int*eresting.' The PR girl shone her eyes at Lucy. When in the conference call the day before, with The Bitch's chairman and the head of the PR agency, words like 'bespoke', 'solvency', 'sustainable income' and 'pro bono' were used, Lucy had said yes to a 'seeing is believing' meeting with someone from the agency this morning. The Bitch was to have a new marketing plan, one that earned it money, and the PR girl had been dispatched to investigate. But because of the boy, Lucy had forgotten the meeting, and she was cross with herself for forgetting. When she had arrived at work this morning, the PR girl was already waiting. They went straight in to it. Lucy ran through The Bitch's history, the people it helped, its services. The PR girl declared her interest. There was no time to ring the hostels, looking for the boy.

'Lanterns are made from tissue paper and willow cane, with tea lights or miniature LED lights inside. All materials are subsidised for anyone on a low-income or on housing support. We get lots of families from different backgrounds now. Some are not necessarily what you'd call middleclass, but can definitely afford to pay the full price. It's an honour system.'

'How *int*eresting.'

'Most still live week to week or month to month not knowing whether they've got work or somewhere to live, how they'll afford to eat or buy food for their kids, or if it's all going to go. They're frightened. They feel hopeless – you can see it in their eyes. If that's your case, the most you're going to pay is four pounds to make a standard-sized lantern.' Holding her palms apart Lucy described a shape. 'Or nothing, if I'm honest. We don't turn anyone away. Everyone else though, everyone else and it's a tenner. On the night itself we've got a team of about six dozen volunteers shaking collection tins and buckets along the parade route and on the seafront. Then, if all twenty thousand spectators each donate just £1 or thereabouts, we'll be okay for a couple of months.'

'*How* interesting.' The PR girl said she would come back to Lucy with a new marketing strategy as soon as she could. Lucy shook her hand and said she couldn't wait.

Lucy listened as someone at the other end of the line tapped at a keypad. It was mid-morning; she was still in her coat and scarf. The Dimplex heater in her office had broken in the night, and the air was frosty. She cradled the receiver between her ear and shoulder so as to hold her mug of tea in both hands. As soon as the PR girl had left, Lucy had started ringing the hostels. None had seen the boy. She had tried half a dozen. Now she was trying the longshots, beginning with St Barts.

'What's that? Yes, at The Bitch. No, tried them already. Them too. I know, I know. About twenty-six, twenty-seven. How what? Not quite...' Lucy, despite having already done so on all of the previous calls, again looked before her to where the boy's eyes would be, and measured upward. 'About five-ten, five-eleven.' She set down her tea and circled round to the front of her desk, as though drawing herself near the boy. She stood facing the spot where she had left him last night. Her heart raced. 'Thin. Brown. Brown. Blue tracksuit bottoms. Dark-grey or even black tweed jacket. Red cravat. Um, heavy cough. Top hat. Yes – a proper one.' Lucy measured its height over her head. She smoothed back her hair, then absently began clearing a patch on the outside edge of her desk on which to perch. Nudging aside a stack of paper files and a wodge of folders, she knocked the newspaper-wrapped bundle to the floor, where it split open. '*What?*'

Three days later, at sunrise, (if it could be called that, for the sun was still so occluded that the streetlights were continuously lit) the haar began to lift. It still held fast a mile or more offshore over The Channel, in the twittens, in the trees and under archways and where the snow had fallen or had blown the deepest, but now there was distance between the land and the sky. At 2 o'clock a slender crack opened in the clouds. Like a spotlight searching for its stage, a blade of sunlight took in the Pavilion, swept slowly to the Corn Exchange, before settling in New Road, near the entrance to the gardens, where Charlotte Reid turned in a circle, screaming for her child. Some five or six paces away Janine Plummer was doing the same and, within a few yards of her, six more mothers and a father were calling in thickening ropes of desperation for their children.

Then, like their children, they heard the Old Man. Without ceremony, without so much as clearing His throat, He had begun softly singing, *Love me, love, me, love me, say you do…*

A crowd formed. Sixty, then eighty, then more. About two dozen of them (including Lucy's friends Wiggy and Edward) aimed their mobile or tablet at and recorded the Old Man. He sang without pause: *It Had to Be You… Things Behind the Sun… Something… Brand New Key… Shut Out the Light… All of You… You Are My Lady…* and everyone stuffed money into the upturned top hat at His feet. Children, sixth formers and university students. English language students. Rockabilly lesbians. Pompadoured gays. Crusties, daytime drinkers, estate agents, stagehands from the theatre across the way, a man in tweed, selling bird whistles. Dogs bolted from their owners, came running and, slavering idiots that they are, knelt, panting. During the chorus to *Believe* the wind lifted a twenty-pound note from the Old Man's hat and sent it sailing above the crowd. There is a photograph of a brittle old biddy leaping a clear two feet off the ground for it: her furled umbrella in the act of dropping, one arm is outstretched from shoulder to gnarled knuckles and fingertips, her eyes popping, mouth almost pornographically agape – and the note, stiff and purple in the wind just beyond her reach in the moment before she catches it. Returning it to His hat, she weighed it down with rings slipped from her fingers, the locket from her neck.

After *Baby I'm a Star*, the Old Man began *Be My Wife* and the wind grew icy and hard. It smelled metallic, like imminent violence. Clouds coiled over the sun and the dark, swollen belly of some great, vituperative beast took form overhead. Moments later it burst, unleashing the snow.

That night in Lucy's dream there was snow and fog. The snow was smooth and thick on the ground and a fog hung in the trees, obscuring the bare branches. In between was the cold, clear air and the tree trunks, black with wet. On the slope of a hillock a short distance ahead was a snow angel. It brought to mind one December, when Lucy was ten or eleven, and she went sledging with friends for three days straight, after school had been called off because of weather. The snow crunches under her feet as she clomps toward the angel. As she nears it she notices someone has pissed over its robes, and that, other than her own, there are no tracks leading to or from the angel itself, just as though it had dropped from the sky and left an impression upon impact. Now beside it, Lucy glimpses herself from below, peering into the angel; then suddenly from above, teetering on the lip of a dark crevice. Bells chime from an old bell tower hidden in the fog, sending birds flying and squawking. Lucy realises she is in a churchyard: amongst the trees are lichen-encrusted stone sarcophagi under thick caps of snow. She feels someone watching her from behind, feels him drawing closer and closer. She runs. Uphill, then along the flat crest, then downhill on an empty Dyke Road. She passes Leopold Road, Albert Road: Seven Dials and home are just ahead. She can't get there fast enough. Running in the snow exhausts her, her boots are weighed down with clumps of it. She skids and slips and glimpses herself from across the street, as though through the eyes of her unseen watcher – and instantly she is outside the churchyard, back where she started, feeling the eyes on her again. Her shoulders prickle and hunch in foreknowledge of uninvited touch. She turns in a circle, but there is no one there. It's night now and the fog is dense. A halo of light filters out from the streetlight ahead.

Below it, she can just about make out a group of people, a shadowy bundle of boys and girls laughing and singing snatches of song. Lucy tells herself she will be safe with them, that they will look after her when they see she is alone (and has lost her mittens). She heads for them. A gust of wind shoves her back. Lucy's legs burn with fatigue, but in a burst she runs hard and makes up some ground. In the fog the group of boys and girls are always dark figures turning another corner, or in the almost reachable distance, weaving in and out of sight. In and out and in and out and in and out – then gone. Lucy realises she stopped hearing their voices some time ago, and now isn't sure where she is. But home feels close; she can sense it. In the near distance she sees a dark figure covered in snow. He is crouched – and the next moment tall and staggering swiftly at her. An old man, eighty or more, in ragged clothes. His mouth is cavernous and panting. The hairs that don't quite ring his head are risen up in the wind like a nest of antlers. At first he is in front of her, in the direction she needs to go to get home. Then he's behind her. Then he's on her shoulders, his fingers in her mouth, his fingers pulling at her teeth, her tongue. Next moment she is home and closing the door. She turns the lock, climbs the final fourteen stairs to her flat, where the lights are already on. When she enters the sitting room, they blink off and stay unlit. Lamplight from the street shines dimly through the windows. When Lucy looks past the sofa to see what's making the pulsing, high-pitched hum, the old man from outside is there, on all fours, his bare ass in the air, scratching appreciatively, almost lovingly, at what she could only describe as an anal tooth.

Like all dreams, Lucy's dream told her something, even if she wasn't sure what. And like many people, Lucy imagined each element of her dream must represent something other than what it was in the dream. The pissed robes: yellow, yellow-bellied – was she scared? What was she scared of? Old man – father? Her father had been avuncular, generous, tweedy, an amateur entomologist and collector of lost words. Elusive and frequently disembodied voices – were they friends she had been too busy to see lately, was one of them the boy (and another one her)? Or did they collectively constitute her animus, the riddling, lyrical spirit of her unconscious? What were they trying to tell her? What had they sung? And the snow angel: white and dropped from high above – was it an egg, was it ovulation, was she in want of a child? Or was it meant to represent a tooth? The tooth...

But it wasn't a dream of allegory or psychoanalytic imagery. Lucy's dream was a dream of arrival and departure. It was a dream of what had happened and what was to come. The Old Man, He was a savage and unnatural devourer.

Upon His arrival in Brighton, church bells (with no bell pullers tugging and bobbing below) sprang into a crazed peal and birds husked into the sky. The birds churned and screamed until, like the haar that would descend in a few days' time, they dropped across the city. The sea rose up and lashed at the pier, at the shore, crashing against and engulfing the hulking cement and stone groynes. Waves smashed through seafront cafés and clubs with a menace multiplied by the swells of sharp shingle shucked up from the beach along the way. Traffic lights blew and the streetlights went, suspending everything in a liminal wintry light. Buses, full in the morning rush, rammed into buildings or collided with each other. Minarets snapped off the Pavilion in the winds and toppled point first, like spears, into the banqueting room below. In St Nicholas Gardens, a florid-faced drunk, caught helplessly in an unbroken two-minute burp, passed out, hit his head, and died.

The Old Man helped himself to the dead man's clothes, then sat on a bench – *In loving memory of Edward and Myrtle* – and considered. He had been somewhere else – and now He was here, wherever here was. He had been somewhere else and then

He was in Denmark Terrace, naked and gasping for air at the bottom of a roadwork pit, a six-foot deep hole, ringed by red and white striped barriers with flashing yellow lights on their corners. There was a foot and a half of cold brown water at the bottom of the hole and its rough walls, revealing strata two centuries old, were slick with mud and dead leaves. Scrabbling out and into the street, He stood and blinked and looked and turned and blinked and looked – first up the road, then down it, toward the sea. As though to somehow aid the divination of His whereabouts, He began to tug meditatively at His scrotum, when—

'Bastard!'

Causing the Old Man to turn just as the sign pole split over (and split open) His head. Casting the broken pole aside, the lollipop lady swung at Him with her fists. The Old Man ran – He ran up Terraces and through Groves, along Places, down twittens, Villas and Roads. He ran without knowing where to run, nor where He was running to (He ran in loops and hoops, in zigs, in zags and, after twenty minutes of running, had run Himself back round to near where He had started). He ran until His knees gave and He fell against the gates of St Nicholas Gardens. Unlocked, the gates swung open and dropped Him on the ground. He fell on His mouth, cracking six teeth top and bottom, of which all but one He left on a stone slab of the garden path, the other tearing the lining of His throat when He involuntarily swallowed. The sea rose. Sirens sounded. Birds circled and screamed. The Old Man turned over and pulled Himself to His knees just as Lucy cycled past the park gates. Bright-eyed, rubicund, thick blonde hair trailing heavily… for a moment, the Old Man felt outside of Himself. For a moment, He was spiked with delight, stupid with delight, and His smile showed every tooth He had left. He blushed. But when He saw where He was (and saw where He was not), saw that the skies roiled in repulsion of Him, that they darkened in disgust of Him, the delight curdled inside of Him and He rotted with despair. He had been somewhere else, somewhere where He had been someone, where He had been *something*. Now it was gone. It was lost. And there was no vision of it, of who and where He had been. It was there only as an absence, a hollowing darkness – darkness and an ever-distancing, plummeting sense of loss. He wept.

That night He caught His reflection in a Sidney Street shop window when a young man shoved Him.

'Fucking watch where you walk.' The young man wore a close-fitting jumper and a checked shirt buttoned to the throat. He smelled of spirits, cigarettes and cologne. 'Fucking old poof.' He turned to see if his friends were watching. There were six others: buttoned up Fred Perrys and Ralph Laurens, gelled hair, drainpipes, vanishing jack-o-lantern grins.

'Fucking *what*?' The young man leaned nearer. 'What you say?'

The Old Man hadn't said anything. Not then, nor at any point since He had arrived. His mouth hung open. Wide-eyed, He took a step back. The young man swung at Him, and missed. The others laughed. The young man turned his head toward his friends and laughed too. The Old Man breathed out. Without looking first, the young man swung and caught the Old Man hard on the mouth, cracking three of His teeth. They fell on the pavement, and the Old Man's head bounced off the shop window in which He'd seen his reflection. 'Boing!' one of the boys hooted in imitation of the sound the glass made.

'Fucking look at him.' The young man pushed his finger off the Old Man's face. 'Bent old queer. Shut your fucking mouth, hanging open like –' he tubed his lips to form a wide O. 'Fucking give you something to put in it. Cocksucking mother—'

'*Kuda b ya ne poshol - tam Ad; ya sam Ad vo ploti,*' the Old Man heard Himself saying. *Which way I fly is Hell; myself am Hell.* The words, though from Him, took form themselves, popping experimentally from His tongue. '*Und,*' He went on, '*in tieffter Tiefe, gröffnet eine tiefre Tiefe.*' *And in the lowest deep, a deeper deep.*

'The fuck? Nah, man, nah. You going to step up to *me*, like that.' Elbows akimbo, the young man pounded his chest with his fists. 'Talk that shit. What you say? What you say to me?'

One of the others lunged forward and punched the Old Man in the ear. He reeled back against the shop window. '*Tam byla má vláda bezpečná. Bohužel i onen nešťastný palác je ztracen. Odsouzen sloužiti v světle a blaženosti. Bída je tvým osudem, pakliže tvůj trůn, třebaže v Pekle, nebude obnoven.*' His eyes were sewn with wild sorrow and dread. *There I but reigned secure. Alas, even that unhappy mansion is lost. Accursed now to serve in beatitude and light. Woe is thy fate, lest thy throne, though in Hell, be restored.*

'Oh that's how it is, is it?' The young man in the checked shirt bounced up and down on his toes like a boxer, throwing purposefully short punches and chanting, 'Here we go. Here we go, here we go.'

The Old Man coughed and a blood bubble formed on His lips. He swallowed and gagged and out came the words sung low, with a touch of scratch: '*Life is just a bowl of cherries…*'

At that, the boy who had hit the Old Man in the ear, punched the boy in the checked shirt to the ground, shoved his hand into the other's pocket and yanked out a roll of banknotes that he tossed to the Old Man. One of the others stepped forward and swiftly beat the ear-puncher in the face, took his wallet and chucked it to the Old Man's feet. Then the next, and the next, until there was only one left. The last one, pudgy as a pup, and with an autograph hunter's look in his eyes, pressed a pound coin into the Old Man's hand, sneezed into tears, turned, and fled.

Around two-thirty that morning, the Old Man let Himself through the twitten door behind 9 Clifton Gardens and from there through the kitchen door. The squatters, asleep on their mattresses, their drugs, their drums and didgeridoos laid down for the night, vanished before dawn. But we got mice. First we had none, then we had many. I caught one, then two, then three, then two more. Then there were none.

It took the Old Man over an hour to tell me about His arrival, and about His nocturnal visit to Lucy at The Bitch three days later. The fire in the Rothenberg's old sitting room burned merrily throughout. I stood transfixed. There is more to the story than I've yet related, and there were bits that tortured Him to say (there was much weeping and many howls). When He had finished (when His finger left me and I was released), I hurried upstairs and bathed vigorously and thoroughly – very thoroughly. Bathing was a difference between the Old Man and me. I did: He didn't.

The Old Man didn't tell me all there was to know. Those things He didn't tell me I picked up through The Glaring. Amongst those who bruited reports about the Old Man and about Lucy were Pepios: an inveterate and assertive gossip who lived with Judith, Lucy's confidant and officer neighbour at The Bitch; Isadore: a logician and reasoner of the first order, but a stunning klutz; Monmouth: a know-it-all and a sneak; Dietrich: scrawny, nerdish, a follower, but honest; Penny: running to fat, manicured and noisy. To hear her speak was like listening to a klaxon. Monkeyboy was a moron and always dirty, dependable, though. He travelled far and wide and I heard from him first or second hand almost daily. Lois: a rare, red beauty with big eyes. Not allowed out, but sometimes sneaked it at night. Reni, who made up for his partial blindness with highly acute hearing. From an open window he could hear people whispering in the café garden three doors away. Fergus, or 'Brains' as we called him: you can imagine him playing six games of chess all at once. Archie, of course. Peregrine, Mimi, Lola, Simeon, Kyoko, Gilou, Jo-Jo, Bix, Daisy Darling, Milton, and Sativa. Sativa, who spoke with a pampered drawl, talked shit, stole, and *unbelievably* got laid.

Long before any of this, Sabrina had been part of it too. Sabrina had something Spanish about her. You could picture her on a Veronese balcony engoldened at sunset, her long, dark hair and pale green eyes half closed as they said apathetically to the clowder of tomcatting suitors below: *Look at me if you must; I don't need you.*

She didn't. She had me. She chose me. Sabrina, if I should meet thee after long years...

* * *

There were three or four inches of snow on every chimney and chimney pot, and two inches along the wires that fanned out spoke-like, above the streets, from telephone poles. Salters and gritters roamed through the night, spraying their load on the fresh-fallen snow, the hard packed snow, the slick sheets of ice. But it wasn't enough; the snow kept coming. So they brought out the snowploughs, behemoths that growled up hills, that rumbled round roundabouts, that snarled along the seafront...

Some time that first week of December, in The Upper Drive and Highcroft Villas, they first uncovered the cracks, the tiny fissures in the road, like a million-strong assembly of hairline dykes threading down from higher ground, toward the sea. There were more in The Drive, in Preston Road, in Egremont Place (and many more yet in the unploughed roads). Those of us with more acute hearing listened in cold fear to the sound of the roads splitting. It was the sound you get when lowering a needle onto a vinyl record. A crackle and hiss, a constant crackle and hiss and pop.

And the air. The air smelled of the sea. It smelled like the precursor, the far-flung microdot spray of an unimaginable wave, gathering behind the heavy curtain of the haar some few miles out over The Channel.

* * *

On 10th December Lucy, instead of going straight to Hadley Place, went along Marine Drive to 'her' bench overlooking the sea. The bench was high above the beach on a walkway bound on one side by the street and on the other by an iron railing and a fifty- or sixty-foot drop to the seafront. Lucy liked to come here before work; watching the sea first thing in the morning was meditative. For some people it was yoga, for Lucy it was watching the sea. But it had been months since she'd had or made the time. This morning the beachfront was still and carpeted with snow; the water, now calm, lapped with weary, unending repetition at the shore. The sea was visible only as a dark body bound to the black mass of the predawn sky. Snowflakes tinselled through the dull orange beams of the street-lights. The occasional car or van crunched cautiously through the snow behind her. And as she sat there, her face muffled nose to chin in the thick bands of her scarf, her mittened hands plunged into her coat pockets and her body hugging in on itself, Lucy's mind searched for something in the sea, the sky, the snow, the quiet, something that would tell her about herself or, at the very least, tell her about today – but it slid into its customary rut: she thought about work (in a little over a week, on the beach before her, under the wary eye of the fleshy-faced frightener who was the Council Health & Safety Officer, two carpenters and a team of Burning of the Clocks volunteers would begin construction of the giant effigy; and three days after that it would be the event itself: the lantern procession, the bonfire and fireworks) and from work her mind leapt to the boy. It had been a week since he had turned up at The Bitch. A week of silence and waiting. This morning, like every morning since the evening she'd found the boy in her office, Lucy reminded herself that he had just shown up, that he had come without warning or appointment. Maybe he would again? Maybe today was the day? Every day for the past week she had been expectant. Every evening the previous week, she had worked late in the hope that the boy might show again at exactly or about the same hour as he had that first and only time. Every night she had returned home with the twin ache of foolishness (she had waited for him and he hadn't shown) and fear (she hadn't waited late enough and had just missed him). She had made arrangements with all of the local hostels to notify her if the boy showed. Every phone call she took and voicemail she retrieved, she hoped would be news the boy had been found, that he was staying at some hostel or another. Every afternoon she rang the hostels just in case they had forgotten to ring her, or had been too busy to tell her the boy was now at theirs. If he was, then what? She didn't have a plan. She knew she would go to him, and that was all.

A pigeon landed on the railing in front of the bench, glanced at Lucy, and flew away. Lucy shivered and thought of a new programme for work: Teaching Inclusiveness, Tolerance & Sensitivity. A quarter of an hour later she was back at her desk, a cup of tea steaming beside her laptop in the frigid office air. She emailed the full programme name of TITS to Wiggy, Belinda, Edward, Bodhi, Anna, and Alan. Wiggy promptly replied to all, proposing a new element to the game: promotional tag – or straplines to go with the programme acronym. TITS: Wiggy offered *Taster Sessions for Beginners* and *Think Big, Feel Better*. Anna submitted *Hands-on Learning*. Belinda pointed out that it should be Hands-on Learning *Experience*, noting that, for best results, you really ought to apply your hands to the tits *and the hole*. Alan challenged everyone with TODGER: *Get a grip*. All of the breakfast shift volunteers had arrived on time. There was apple and cinnamon porridge, banana pancakes, tofu sausages, and fresh fruit to eat. It was a fine morning.

'Just come and look at this. No? You're certain? Well, I'll tell you what I see. There's a boy down there.'

Lucy shot up from her desk chair, and froze. The Council Health & Safety Officer's hands were clasped behind his back and he wore an expression of benevolent innocence. He returned his attention out of the window and continued, 'He's about...' he waggled his head. 'Oh, I'd put him at about eleven or twelve-years-old, and his entire left side is covered in snow, even his poor little bobble-hatted head. But do you know *why* his entire left side is covered in snow? Do you want to guess? No? I'll tell you why his entire left side is covered in snow. He fell on his way to your door.'

Lucy said nothing, and sat down again. It was ten o'clock and the Council Health & Safety Officer, unlike the PR girl the previous week, had turned up without an appointment. He came, he told Lucy when he announced himself with a verbalised 'knock-knock' once he was already through her office door, 'just for a chat'. He came, he had said, plucking his gloves off finger by finger 'on spec'. Leaving Lucy to half-wonder if she was to blame for his visit. Only hours earlier, he had crawled to mind while she was looking over the dark and frozen seafront. Could that, like a ricocheted radio transmission, have bounced its way to him, prompting his visit? The Council Health & Safety Officer's ears were red.

'I myself almost did the same on my way in.' He tutted, and considered his boots. 'Yes, I'm afraid I must say it. Yes, and the floor downstairs at reception is virtually a pool of half-melted – Oh dear. Dear, oh dear. No, don't be cross. And breathe. Calm. *Calm.* And breathe. We can count to ten if you like.'

Beaking his mouth and then popping his lips apart a few seconds later the Council Health & Safety Officer went on. 'But I didn't come here to talk to you about your building. Methinks with a little initiative you can see to all of that this very morn. No, I came here to talk to you about the week after next. The Burning of the Clocks. No. Hear me out, Miss Cuthman. Hear me out. If a boy – a healthy boy of eleven or twelve – can go falling down and get himself covered in snow whilst trotting happily along to your door in the mid-morning – no, we shan't call it "sun", but light, daylight – if a healthy boy of eleven or twelve can go falling down in the midmorning daylight, just imagine what will happen the week after next, when there are – how many is it, *twenty thousand*? Just imagine what will happen the week after next when we have *twenty thousand* people, many of them drinking, of that I have little doubt, drinking and smoking their *reefers*, and all of those children marching in freezing temperatures after dark, just imagine the potential for...' The Council Health & Safety Officer winced. He shook his head. He sighed. 'The sheer scale of it keeps me awake nights. Just imagine the sheer scale of injuries. Just imagine the cost.'

Lucy didn't need to imagine the cost. No Burning of the Clocks meant no staff and volunteers rattling collection buckets and tins – a twenty thousand pound loss. The Bitch needed it. The Bitch depended on it. Meaning there was a higher, more damaging cost. No twenty thousand pounds meant cutting services for homeless families, and cutting jobs. Human costs. But the financial cost was a firm, calculable figure, and all that Lucy could articulate to herself just then. Meeting the Council Health & Safety Officer's eyes, Lucy said, 'So what you're telling me is that you're going to call it off?'

The Council Health & Safety Officer inhaled sharply and his hand flew to his heart. On his face was a look of horrified innocence. 'No. Oh no. Not me. *You.*'

Lunch that day was a cup of instant tomato soup, four ginger nuts, the post and emails. In the post were a red-topped notice for an eighteen hundred pound unpaid bill from the plasterers who had started on the ground floor loos and then not shown for three weeks, and four funding rejections, each for between fifteen and twenty-five thousand pounds. There were two more rejections by email, for a total of thirty thousand pounds. The Council Health

& Safety Officer had given Lucy one week. If the winds were still strong, if there was more snow, if there was ice, if the cracks in the streets spread near the seafront, if the temperature wasn't above… One week, the Council Health & Safety Officer told her. The Council Health & Safety Officer – that was a good one. CHSO. Cosh.

At 19:20, Lucy looked out of her office window. Then she turned out the lights, set the alarm, locked the front door, and left.

As you neared home you crossed the street near the big metal dumpster where you had fallen the week before. The mound of rubbish that was piled around the dumpster had been cleared that afternoon. But now there was an old standard lamp (with a scalloped and tasselled shade) leant against the dumpster. Next to it was a sofa. The sofa was evidently only recently dumped: like the rug that had broken your fall last week (which, unfurled beneath the mound of rubbish as it had been, was now glued with ice to the street) it was darkly luciferous beneath a dusting of snow. One of the sofa's armrests jutted into the street beyond the dumpster, where it could punch at the sliding cars, where it could thump the sloshing buses, the slaloming lorries. You could have just walked on by. You could have just hurried across the street, indoors and upstairs to cup of tea, a toastie and telly. But you had to stop and nudge the sofa closer to the kerb with your hip. When it wouldn't budge, you spun all the way round and bopped it with your bum. Nothing. Using both your hands you gave it a solid shove. One of the sofa legs caught against something, snapped, sending the whole thing listing backward, and knocking the standard lamp upright. The sofa leg had caught against a plastic takeaway bag, stuffed and knotted at the top. You booted the bag toward the dumpster, where it split open. A twenty pound note flopped out and, like a landed fish, flipped across the rug. You caught it under your boot on the third go.

And standing there, your heart rising to your throat, the takeaway bag spilling its guts to you in the tidy little suite of the rug, the sofa, the lamp (the tassels of its scalloped shade swaying), you think you hear it again, this time sounding through the clacking branches of the bare trees overhead: *Home.* Only now it's not lowed or moaned. It is whispered. A plangent *Home. Home. Home.*

* * *

'Come on. Oh, *come on*. John Lee Hooker.' Long-limbed and long-faced beneath a sidelocked Mod haircut, Wiggy's head jutted forward and back like an egret's.

'Nope. Jackie Wilson. I'm telling you. Or… hang about. Maybe it was Aretha?'

'Same version. Try listening to the lyrics next time. Berry Gordy Jr – you may have heard of him, made a name for himself with a little label called Motown? – Berry Gordy Jr wrote them. John Lee Hooker's is a different song altogether. And better. And I want you to pay attention to me now, Edward. It's because I love you – yes, yes… *yes* – and I can't stand seeing you go around making a tit of yourself. At home is one thing. Knock yourself out. But here, in front of everyone…' with an upturned palm, Wiggy, in the manner of a game show host displaying a prize, traced a semi-circle around the table at Lucy, Bodhi, Alan, Anna and Belinda. 'The songs went – when we got there the old boy already had a crowd around him, but from when we got there the songs went: *Mighty Mighty Man*.' Wiggy listed on his fingers, beginning with his thumb. '*Disorder*. No, *So You'll Aim Toward the Sky*, then *Disorder*. *Ring My Bell*. A fucking epicedial *Be My Baby* – you were in pieces, which is probably why you can't get it through your bulbous mule head that what came next was *I'm Wanderin'*, the John Lee Hooker version.'

Outside the wind blew hard along the street and the hinged pub sign above the front door was tilted in the wind and creaked when the wind momentarily let up, before blowing hard again. The pub's ground floor windows were fogged with the breath of everyone inside and from the pair of log and coal fires that burned, one in the front and the other in the back of the pub. The ceilings were low and greying yellow in colour and there was bunting of ivy and of silver and red tinsel and of pine on the greying yellow walls. The only light came from the three or four wall sconces with small, flame-shaped bulbs and the candles on the dozen or so tables and on the bar, the low-burning fires, and what light filtered through the windows from the tall and arced streetlight further along Foundry Street.

'But have I played it for you? No? Wait. Wait. You've got to see this. Both times. It's – it's *fucking weird*. I've seen him – this old boy – three times now. It's always complete chance. First time my mobile was dead, but last week, and then again the other day with Old Cloth Ears here.' Wiggy tipped his head at Edward and scrolled a thumb across his mobile screen. There were speakers on hooks, high in the corners of the room. *Metal Guru* was playing; before that it had been *Blackwaterside*. 'No. No. *No*. Got all these photographs of tourists taking photographs of themselves in front of graffiti murals. There's a coffee table book in it. Why do they do it? Why do they do it *so much*? Look at this one. You've got to laugh. I mean, check *him* out. Oversized specs – tick. Drainpipes – tick. Six-inch turn-ups – tick. Hip-hop hightops. Baseball cap askew. Here all the way from Christ knows where.' Wiggy flicked his wrist backward.

'Valencia.' Anna reached over and, plucking the phone from Wiggy, widened the onscreen image with her fingers. 'See the bat logo in the folds of his scarf?' She made it wider yet. 'There. And the red and gold bands.'

'Or Tokyo or Sao Paulo or wherever.' Wiggy took the phone back and resumed scrolling along the screen. 'And you're knocking around Brighton car parks, taking turns pouting in front of Mandela's head or Gargamel or whatever, to bore everyone with at home. Banksy. No. No. *No.* Yes. Now here.' Wiggy set his mobile screen face up on the table. Everyone leaned forward, other than Edward, who'd already seen it and was rolling a cigarette. Mimi stretched and yawned at the fire. They were in the front room, at a table below the windows, with the fireplace at one end and the front door at the other.

'This is him in New Road last Friday. Gardens are there. Corn Exchange is just to the left. We were off to the side and back a bit. But you could hear him clear. He was singing Nick Drake.'

'*Time Has Told Me.*' Edward winked at Lucy.

'Wrong again. Jesus. And I'm supposed to spend Christmas with you. It was *Time of No Reply*. But it doesn't matter, because if I just —' Wiggy turned up the volume and a skirling metallic screech had everyone covering their ears. 'That's him,' Wiggy shouted over the noise. 'That's what I got of him singing.' He turned it off. 'But then.' He scrolled the video forward. 'But then this.' This time you could hear a voice, syncopated, almost chanting. But the words were garbled and swallowed back into themselves. The volume swelled and fell and swelled and fell and the gulped back words gradually grew faster and were joined by an unintelligible, sibilant whispering.

'That's him singing Bowie, fifteen, twenty minutes later. But look at him. He's there; you can see him, right? But you can't make him out. Not clearly. Her, you can, that girl there when she comes up to give him money. Look: ten, ten, fiver – you can actually make out the notes. And that fellow in the flat cap. Her with the earmuffs. Him in the nose ring. That granny. But the old boy himself – no. The air in front of him's always smudged. It's rippled. He fucking stank to high fucking heaven, I can tell you. But it's like he actually curries the air. Can't be my phone either. All the stuff I did before and since works a treat.

'Apart from this.' Wiggy shook his head. 'This is two days ago, right. We'd bumped into Jon and Dom on their way to meet Bex and them, at the Basketmakers. But when we got down the bottom of Gloucester Road there was a crowd. The old boy's there in the centre, with sixty or seventy people listening to him sing. I've ballsed it up before, so I'm going to get it this time. I mean live he's got a beautiful, beautiful voice. Gave him all my money that time in New Road. I must have had thirty-something quid on me too. Fucking fortune. That's what it's like. I didn't even look. Just, here – take it, take it all. But listen.' Wiggy turned up the volume. 'Hear it? He turned up the volume more and scrolled the video forward, at random. The sound was the same. 'And here.' He scrolled forward again. 'And here'. It was the sound of a little girl giggling – giggling coquettishly. 'Him. Same wherever you listen – *that's him*. But here's what really spooks me.' Wiggy cast his eyes at everyone around the table. 'Take a close look at him. It's dark, I know. The resolution's not great. And we're twenty-five, thirty feet away, so you can't really make out the hairs on his head wriggling up like…' Wiggy held up a hand to the back of his head and wriggled his fingers in the air. 'But *it is* the back of his head, isn't it? You see it. Big. Bald. No nose. No eyebrows. No mouth. But look.' Wiggy's voice began to quiver. 'See the red cravat around his neck, see how it's knotted? It's like it's at the front. And his shirt collar – there – right collar, left – like it's the front. And his jacket lapel, open like at the front. And his hands, if I freeze it – there, you see – crooked up like a stick insect. He was facing us. We were facing him. But where do you see his face?'

When at the pub Lucy told everyone about the money she'd found beside the dumpster, and that instead of keeping it she'd deposited it into The Bitch's bank account, she thought she felt a collective (and collectively stifled) wince. Edward could have used it for; Belinda would have put it towards; Bodhi would have; Alan needed to; Anna could have done with; Wiggy *really* had to... But back at her flat later that evening, telling Flip was different. 'That and the newspaper parcel. That makes...hmmm.' Lucy scooped up Flip and kissed him on the nose. Flip stretched out on his back. His forepaws were cocked like a rabbit's, and his hindpaws were extended straight out over Lucy's arm, toes splayed in delight. 'You're smart. What's eight thousand four hundred and twenty-five plus three thousand one hundred and twenty-four? No, three thousand one hundred and *thirty-eight*. Three one three eight, that's right. Think it's right. Something like that. What's eight four two five and three one three eight?

'Tell you. It's not half what we need. Not a quarter. But is good. Every bit. Specially if they want to cancel it. Health n' Safety man said *I'm* to do it. Ha! Me. Card came with it, the plassic bag. Said "At this festive time of year – something, something – for the poor an destitute who suffer greatly at the present time." Know that one? Dickens. And I found it – the money in the parcel was at work, but the money in the plassic bag and card was rydunere. Show you.'

Lucy carried Flip to the window. Only the fairy lights surrounding it were lit. The rest of the flat was dark in defiance of the creeping unease Lucy had felt walking home from the pub. She had left alone. A solitary figure stood at the far end of the street, away from the direction Lucy was heading. He stood in the middle of the street, perfectly still, perfectly dark against the white folds of snow, with his head bowed. Lucy looked at the figure for a moment, pulling her scarf and hat tight against the icy wind. Even though she couldn't make him out, Lucy could feel his eyes on her. Minutes later, in Upper Gloucester Road, she heard footsteps scrabbling up behind her. She turned to look; whoever it had been, she told herself, must have turned off onto the side street, or gone indoors. But further along, in Alexandra Villas, she again sensed someone watching her, a presence, and was certain she heard her name, a call so hoarse and raw it was as though it was scratched on the wind. When she looked, she thought she saw a lone figure standing at the far end of the street, between snow enfolded cars. And then, near Compton Avenue, came the sound of footsteps crunching slowly, slowly behind her...

All the talk at the pub had done it, she told herself. She'd allowed it to spook her. The dark skies, the drinks, and the talk. After Wiggy had finished telling everyone about trying to record the old man singing, Lucy had told everyone about her dream. The snow angel. The tolling bells and dark pit. The sense of being watched, of being chased. Voices in the fog. The old man waiting for her in the dark. She hadn't told them about his tooth. But she told Flip about it when she got in. 'Keep the lice off, she'd said. ''Cept these.' She turned on the fairy lights around her front window. 'Be brave.' She burped. 'Such a lightweight. Three glasses of wine and look at me. Oops, and a brandy. Mixed, that's why. Dutch courage. Brave now. No lice, 'cept these. Had the craziest dream the other night, And ryhere, Flip. Right. Here.' She pointed at the grass-like rug in front of the sofa. 'He was ryehere. Scabby, naked, old saggy wrinkled arse old man, *scratching at it*. Making a noise like he was...' And Lucy told Flip what she had seen. And Flip listened.

'And rydunere,' she told Flip now. He was in her arms and his high watt purr vibrated against her chest. 'We'll sing White Christmas after this. And food. You like food, don't you, Flip? We can eat some prawn crackers and... whatever else we got. Tuna. You like your tuna. *I* like *my* tuna. But it was rydunere, under that sofa, there beside the dumpster. See it? Look. Still there for three days. Be there for an age. Ages and ages. Probably forever. Rydunere, beside the dumpster. You can see it clearly in —' Lucy blinked. Her sitting room windows were frosty and the drinks had been on an empty stomach, but from the standard lamp (from behind its scalloped and tasselled shade) beside the dumpster, she was certain she could see a faint glow of light.

The cracks in the streets, the tiny threadlike fissures, metastasised. They spread unchecked in the dark, when the temperature had fallen, when curtains and shutters were drawn against the cold. In Upper Rock Gardens, they sped from the street and up the walk of a house and pulled its face off. They shattered the spine of Hampton Street and cracked across the brow of eight or nine of its terraces like black lightning. Everyone had to evacuate before dawn. In Brunswick Road, Montpelier Road, Regent Hill and Manor Hill, they pulled apart the road like carded wool. The new cracks were different than those that had first appeared. They were the same hairline slits or incisions, only now they had miniature labellate ridges to them. And the sound they made had changed. It was no longer the crackle and hiss of a needle on an old album. Now it was a whispering – the ultrasonic, cacophonous whispering of millions.

* * *

The carpeting in Belinda's stairwell was tea-stained and wine-stained and worn. It was held together by gaffer tape in a way that made it look like a long, elbow-patched sleeve. The walls alongside and at the top of the stairs (like the sitting room, the bedroom, the hallway, the box room) were woodchipped and crowded skirting board to cornice with framed and unframed artwork. Watercolours, aquatints, photogravures, woodcuts, pencil drawings, postcards and posters from Mucha, Hoffman, Moll, Mackintosh and many more. Every few feet there were blank spaces, usually with a nail or hook and a dust outline marking where a picture had hung before Belinda had sold it. Some of the works were originals and when one of these sold, it earned Belinda enough money to buy weed or hash and to scour car boot sales and charity shops for two or three new pieces of lost provenance. These she would clean up and sell at a modest profit through the eBay shop that she ran out of her box room, and for which the flat itself was the warehouse. Aside from the kitchen, with its facinorous drains and the fresh breeze that blew through the draughty window onto the little yard at the back, the flat smelled of sebum, pine, bergamot oil, and ashtrays.

Between the fireplace and the front bay window was a stuffed armchair with a curved back and high armrests. It had the best view of the front room, and it was where, on Christmas Eve, I had been dozing when Belinda came and sat on the floor below me.

'How goes it, Old Bean?' Belinda's hair was bunched atop her head like a fountain and her face was flushed. She had been cleaning since before dark and now it was past dinner time. First she had smoked a spliff (she had sold a pair of Kampmanns, and anyway it was Christmas), then a cuppa, and then got to work. The recycling had been humped down the street: bottles, cans, jars, newspapers, old unopened post. The cooker scoured. The bog brushed. The sinks scrubbed. The teetering towers of books on the dining table and on the floor had been pushed onto shelves or broken into shorter stacks and wedged between the armrests of the stuffed chairs and the sitting room floor, or bundled up to the bedroom. The floors hoovered, the sofa and the stuffed chairs hoovered, the floors mopped, the fireplace swept. Laundry dried on radiators and from the pulleyed airing rack above the bath. I'd taken a long and proper bath and hoped Belinda would remember to change the bedclothes.

'What are we going to do with you, eh? What are we going to call you?' For a moment I thought she was going to try and kiss me, but instead she began tidying up the records. Several had been left lying about; Belinda took some time looking at each and turning them over to look at the back cover, then the front again, sometimes taking them out to read the lyrics on the sleeves, when there were any, and sometimes humming or singing aloud for a moment or two as she skinned up, lit up, built a fire, opened an ale, and played songs from the records that had been left about, or slid the records into the old wine crates below the turntable and pulled out others. She played *The Fox in the Snow*, *Since Yesterday*, *Just What I've Always Wanted*, *The Universal*, the *Sanctus* and *In Paradisum* from *Faure's Requiem*. Belinda finished the ale, made peppermint tea and smoked another spliff. We listened to *Brandenburg Concertos* Nos 2 and 4, and the full A side of *His n' Hers*. I had a terrific itch behind my ear, so I scratched it.

Belinda had good, almost feline instincts. She understood when I wanted company and when to leave me alone. At 9 Clifton Gardens, I could feel the Old Man's eyes following me like a painting. Even when He was in a different room, or when we were on separate floors of the house and all of the lights were off, I felt His eyes on me. It was only when I went down the twitten and around the corner, to sit at Sabrina's graveside, or to find something to eat that I felt unobserved.

Eating was never the same after Sabrina died. Now it was something I did alone, always hurried and almost always takeaways. Sabrina and I... we had made certain we ate together at least once a day. Sabrina was the more finicky of us. She loved poultry, but not so much fish, and only very occasionally red meat. Eggs, yes, but only if they were poached or boiled, and never any cheese. She was wild about wood pigeon; with me it was sardines. Sabrina couldn't have kids – but I didn't mind. Sometimes I think she did though. Sometimes she over-ate to forget, to send her to sleep. Sometimes I think she could have slept for days. Some days she was sulky and bored when I found and woke her, and I had my work cut out for me trying to cheer her out of her mood. Sometimes it was easy, and all she needed was a game (she could race – *oh*, could she race). But then she got knocked down in Dyke Road one August afternoon when I was lazing about in the garden at home. I heard her cry and came running. There wasn't anything I could do. And the car – the car didn't even stop. There was no one around. She was alone. I wish there had been a final goodbye, that she'd blinked at me and I'd blinked at her, that we kissed each other with our eyes. I tried attending the funeral (she was given a home burial), but her family ran me off. I couldn't think of what to do. So I climbed a tree I'd never climbed before and sat in it for a long, long while.

On one of my last nights at Clifton Gardens, I was feeling maudlin and came close to asking the Old Man for a song. I had wandered out for something to eat and eventually tucked into a lamb donar (Sabrina would have turned away with a sniff and a sneeze) and gathered the latest news from The Glaring. When I got home, I found the Old Man had kicked down the banister and pulled up half the floorboards that had lined the front hall and torn everything to pieces. You could see straight down, past the joists and into the cold cellar. A fire – the only light throughout the house – blazed in the front room. I found Him crouched on the floor in front of it, holding His knees in His arms and weeping. The infuriated, frustrated cries of an infant. I had the feeling He knew when I'd be home, but it didn't stop Him wailing. It was only after He saw that I had settled myself in front of the fire and was blinking at its warmth that He, adjusting His ball sack, raised himself to His feet and hawked into the flames. Hard, pebble-like snow prattled against the steel shutters on the windows and the wind whistled oboe-like through their perforations. I thought about how things might have been if Sabrina was here and the Rothenbergs were at home. She would come round for a second tea, and there'd be music. I wanted more than anything right then to hear *What'll I Do*. But I knew it would do me no good to ask.

The heart-shaped shit. It puzzled me. Had He left it on purpose? Was it for me? And, if not for me (and not for Him), for whom? Turning this over in my mind, I found my way to a much more difficult question: *Whose was it?*

* * *

On the morning the city council was to decide if the Burning of the Clocks could go ahead, or if Lucy would be forced to cancel it, Lucy sat at her desk proofing The Bitch's quarterly newsletter. The newsletter was put together with contributions from staff and volunteers and from the homeless and unemployed who used the centre. Reading it aloud helped Lucy spot mistakes. 'Their' for 'there'. 'Are' for 'our'. 'Continual' for 'continuous'. 'BITCH' for 'BHITC'. And so on. Its publication had been postponed until it was known whether or not Burning of the Clocks was cancelled. Lucy had drafted an emergency fundraising appeal for the newsletter's front page in case it was called off. If it was still going ahead, however, construction of the giant effigy on the seafront would begin tomorrow. This year's effigy was of Father Time rendered as a grandfather clock. Lucy amused herself by sketching the clock face to feature that of the Council Health & Safety Officer. In the week since he had visited, there had been new snow and it remained biting cold, especially when the winds whipped south from the Downs. Streets split and splintered. There had been no news about the boy. Lucy struggled to keep her hopes up. The cheeriness she wore had begun to rust.

By midday, things had worsened. The skies, which had been bright and clear, turned dark. Clouds crashed in like wrestlers leaping in from the ropes and laid down a stiff sheet of hail. The PR girl emailed Lucy the new marketing strategy; it would cost £35,000 over each of the next two years. She said she hoped cost wasn't an issue. The pipes in the ground floor loos burst and an emergency plumber had to be summoned. Lucy's lunch was a cup of instant cauliflower soup and a satsuma whilst covering for the lantern-making instructor who had crashed his car on the ice.

The lantern-making workshop was busy, at least; and it wasn't until Michaela returned from lunch and relieved her, that Lucy could check for messages about the boy or from the city council. The council had convened at two that afternoon and the Council Health & Safety Officer had tabled a motion to force cancellation of the Burning of the Clocks. At 14:14 he suddenly stopped mid-sentence and, vaulting over the table from which he had been presenting, rushed to the window, threw it open and beckoned the councillors to: 'Just come and listen to this.'

That wo is me, pore childe, for thee
And ever morne and may
For thy parting neither say nor sing
Bye Bye...

The city council crowded round the windows and listened as the singing swelled. Outside, in Bartholomew Square, the Old Man sang a medley: *In the Bleak Midwinter... The Boar's Head Carol... Do You Hear What I Hear... This Endris Night.*

'Huzzah! Huzzah!' the Council Health & Safety Officer heard himself cry when the Old Man had finished. The city council – all forty-six in attendance that day – applauded. The motion to cancel Burning of the Clocks was instantly and unanimously scrapped. 'Hark, hark!' the Council Health & Safety Officer called out through the open window. And the city councillors' money flew and fluttered from the windows to the snowy square below, where it was fetched up by the crowd of eighty or more who piled it in and then around the Old Man's upturned top hat.

At 17:17, Meg, who volunteered at reception, burst into Lucy's office breathless and beaming. 'This!' And she showed Lucy the bin liner brimming with pound notes and Euros and the colourful currencies of three continents. Lucy flew past her, through Judith's and Michaela's office, through Lauren's, through the short hallway narrowed in half by a bank of filing cabinets and down the stairs, two at a time, to reception, in hope that the boy was still there.

* * *

'That's Jarvis over there,' Belinda said. 'He's traumatised, so let him sleep. I'll properly introduce you when he wakes. Now then. You're clinking like a bottle bank in a windstorm. What treasures have you brought? Armagnac – oh, *lovely*. Lager. More lager. More…stout and – No! Lambrusco! I haven't had that since uni. *Now* it's Christmas. We'll just pop it in the makeshift fridge.' Belinda opened the French doors to the little yard at the back. I peeped across when I felt the cold breeze. Edward saw me looking, winked and smiled. 'A very happy Christmas to you, sir.'

Wearing a tweed waistcoat, tweed tie, tweed trousers, long sideburns and with his moustache curled ever slightly upward at the ends, Edward looked Edwardian. Only the gap between his two front teeth somehow made it seem a joke, and like he was many years younger than he was.

'Right. Champers there nearest the door.' Belinda pointed outside. That morning, after wrapping presents, she had forged a path through the snow to the wooden bench that was fixed to the wall below the kitchen window. The bench was heaped with snow, and poking from it, like a glass orchard, was an array of green and brown bottles. 'White wine. Ale. Porter. Baileys. Fizzy water at the far end. Reds are in the kitchen. Alan's bringing the whisky. Now then. Thirsty?'

The lights in the front room were low and the fire in the grate warmed my nose and toes. Outside, on the pavement, the snow squeaked beneath the feet of the passers-by. The sky was brown with cloud and, inside, the fairy lights twinkled in the bough of long-needled pine, affixed to the ceiling where a wall had once separated the rooms. Belinda put on Phil Spector's Christmas album. Edward pushed a log onto the coals. It crackled and spat and caught flame. Anna peeled a clementine and gave half to Alan. Bodhi set about rolling a six-paper spliff. Everyone had drinks, and everyone but Wiggy was there. Wiggy had texted he was running late, but Lucy... No one knew yet that she wasn't coming. No one knew she was missing, that she'd been lost for practically as long as I'd been found.

'Dead posh up there, Clifton Gardens.' Belinda flicked the dog-end of her roll-up into the fire. 'But, like I said, I could hear him crying from the far end of the street. When I got close, I could see he was shaking with cold. His face was scratched and there were clumps of blood on his head and clumps of his hair in the snow around him. I didn't know whether he'd been attacked or if he'd done it to himself or what. We were on the park side of the street; he was staring at a house across the way. I knelt down and asked him if he was all right and he looked at me like he had something to say but – there. Look. That look.'

Everyone turned and looked at me. I had raised my head to say something. My mouth was open; now I closed it.

'What else could I do? It was getting dark. There was no one around. I took him home.'

Listening to Belinda tell it made it worse. I was here, and Lucy... You'd think I'd be grateful, and in a way I suppose I was. When Belinda found me three days before Christmas, I was near frozen, hungry and confused. My house – the house where I had first opened my eyes, whose stairwell I had raced up and down, in whose windows I had watched for the rain to end or followed the blackbirds as they swooped to and from the bay tree in the front garden, the house where I had slept months of hours, where on holidays I had scoffed milk-poached salmon, guinea fowl, braised brisket, roast goose and roast duck, the house where I had listened in closed-eye bliss to the Rothenbergs singing and playing music – had vanished. I had known the creak of every floorboard and in which corner of every room the sun shone and when. I knew the year-round autumn leaf scent of the shed (once an outhouse) in the back garden, the deep rich pong of the flowerbeds front and back, knew hard and well to avoid the wasps that spun drunkenly when in October the damsons fell to the ground beside the twitten door, knew that the front hall radiator sounded in the key of b when switched on again after a summer of unuse, and how a tube of Pringles being opened in the kitchen could be heard from the second floor landing. The house was double-fronted, with a slate-tiled kitchen at the back, William Morris wallpaper in the stairwell, three bedrooms on the first and second floors, and a loft where half a symphony of old and damaged instruments (bashed bassoons, crumpled cornets, an unstrung, pillarless and de-pedalled harp), picture frames, suitcases and stacks of old magazines grew dusty around the clapped-out corduroy sofa where Margaret Rothenberg, in the year before she died, liked to sequester herself to recompose the dots to the string quartet she'd written when she was seventeen, and where I, since when I was very young, liked to nap when I was feeling queasy or had a cold. And now all of it was gone. First He came. Then Lucy followed him home. And on the night of Burning of the Clocks, on the darkest day of the year...

The night air smelled of coal fire and wood smoke. Beneath the slices of sky between the two and three storey buildings of The Lanes were strings of lights and beneath the lights was snow and beneath the snow the dark red brick of the narrow passageways, and above all of it were snow clouds drifting across the black sky and the curved claw of the moon. Lucy weaved hurriedly through The Lanes, toward the bit of kerbside in East Street where she always watched the Burning of the Clocks procession of lanterns and drum troops and dancers. It was where she had, years earlier, seen her first Burning of the Clocks and she returned to the same spot every year. Belinda would meet her there. Together they would watch the procession pass by and would travel with the final wave of lantern bearers along the seafront roadway to the beach, where all of the lanterns were piled beneath the giant effigy, and then the pyre would be lit and the effigy would burn high into the night sky and the fireworks would burst red and blue and gold over the sea.

It had snowed that afternoon and Lucy had been called to the seafront for a final health and safety inspection of the bonfire and firework site. Cold and wet had seeped through her boots and after the inspection she had needed to hurry back to The Bitch to finish work, and then from The Bitch, home, for a dry pair of boots before meeting Belinda in East Street. Now the thing to do was to get there before the crowds grew thick and Lucy would be stuck somewhere at the back, away from Belinda and unable to view from the kerbside the procession she had almost been forced to cancel.

At 19:19 you checked your phone. Belinda was still not there and the Burning of the Clocks procession had begun. A battery of drummers was playing hard and the booming of the big bass drums and the higher rat-a-tat of the snares and tamborims beat out a hard samba. The crowd on the pavement either side of the street was four and five deep. Those in the back were flat against the darkened shop fronts and some filled the shop front doorways. People stood on tiptoes and there were children on shoulders and the people at the front stood on the kerb. Underfoot, on the pavement, there was snow, packed hard and brown with grit. The street itself had been cleared of snow and salt crystals sparkled beneath the streetlights. Ghostly plumes from everyone's breath rose above the crowd and hovered and vanished and were instantly replenished.

The procession was long and filled the tight streets of narrow three and four storey buildings with shops on the ground floor that were closed for the night. At the front of the procession was a cascading troop of women dancers, with blacked out eyes and skeleton teeth outlined in black on their white-painted faces, who wore white ruffles tight around their necks, huge skeletal fairy wings on their backs and long, hooped and rigid white skirts with cut-outs that revealed flashes of leg. Some wore skeleton costumes and those who did lurched forward jerkily, as though their joints were uncoupling and their limbs disjointing and re-jointing as they staggered and glided forward. Next came the first wave of two hundred or more white-glowing lanterns, shaped like domes and globes and stars and those that were owl-shaped or shaped like human torsos and human heads and animal heads and antlered creatures and many sizes of bells. The drums boomed louder and the two-handed metal rattles shook and sounded off the buildings with people in the windows, looking down from the higher floors and waving glowing lanterns in the cold night air.

Turbaned Sikhs with curled black and silver moustaches and sequined vests and pantaloons marched militarily forward with lanterns and banners, followed by spinning women dancers in dark, silk robes and silvery bat-like wings that spun outward and rippled from their outstretched arms and from long wands held in their hands, and a tall tottering of stilt-walkers ten and twelve feet high, wearing white and black-striped leggings and jackets and with white-painted faces and blacked out eyes and black lips.

Then another two hundred or more lanterns that were crescent-shaped, house-shaped and diamond-shaped and dome- and globe-shaped. These had silhouettes of crows and wolves and large hearts and flying gulls and flickering black flames and clusters of miniature hearts and stars. The banging tambourines and the drums which had been around the corner now poured into the street and the samba grew loud from the sixty or more drummers now in sight and all playing in unison and the towering wave of sound hit you from the drummers all dressed in black and with faces painted white and with stiff black cat whiskers or white with thick horizontal black bars. All wore black top hats or bowler hats and many had foot-long paper-mâché legs in black and white striped leggings and black high heels frozen in upside down can-can kicks affixed to the top of them. The drummers beat their drums and were high-stepping and crouching and back-arching in unison, their black and white-painted faces unreadable and their identities indiscernible in the black and white face paint and the black clothing and black bowler hats and the tall, black, top hats.

Behind the drummers were more drummers and in between were more lanterns on poles, six and eight feet long and held high in the air by stiff cane poles or bobbing backward in the wind and up again and down and back and up and down, on slender willow poles, bopping in wild time to the sambas being beat by the two batteries of drummers, each trying to play louder and harder than the other the heavy-booming bass drums that you could feel in your stomach and made your heart race and your eyes hot. The drums heave and are bass heavy and the high constant patter of the brassy snares and tamborims together shake the shop windows and the drummers break cleanly from the samba and all together, like a flight of cannoned starlings, swerve into a military beat as though they are the vanguard of an army steaming into battle.

When suddenly the drumming stops and there is a quick silence before the crowds on both sides of the street, now five and six deep in places, cheer and then a lone drummer kicks up again and the cowbell players find it and then the bass drummers and the snare drummers and tamborim drummers and tambourine shakers take it and in seconds it's heaving and glacier heavy and there are dancers swirling and leaping and the lanterns are bobbing and the windows rattling and the pavement crowd hip-thrusting and shoulder-swinging and fevered in the cold wind and you are in the thick of it and moving your hips and your shoulders to the new samba when you see a lone top hat in the crowd across the street, turning away from you and you are certain it's the boy and there is nothing that matters now but the boy and you and the boy.

You squeeze into the street and skirt through the overspilling crowd, looking for gaps through the parade to the other side of the street. You look for the boy's top hat and you find it and you push through a family and then a clutch of students drinking from bottles of wine and brandy and you see the boy across the street again and you push past more onlookers and look again and a flood of two hundred white-glowing lanterns are flowing past on bobbing willow poles and erect cane poles, lanterns horseshoe crab-shaped and jellyfish-shaped, with long dangling bits, and squid-shaped and oarfish shaped and shaped like boats and clock faces and the four-faced, golden-domed clock tower in the city centre.

You can't see beyond or through the wave of lanterns. You jump and look and jump and look and find him and when you jump again Belinda spots you and pushes out of the doorway where she was forced to a standstill on her way to meet you. She calls for you but the drums are hammering down the street and now there is a shrill whistle from the street and a new battle of the drum troops begins and the new troop is trying to outplay the one that just passed and the new one of forty or more drummers have whistles sounding and trombonists blatting. Belinda pushes toward you, but the crowd is too thick and doesn't part and by the time she reaches where you were, you have pushed into the street and are hurrying against and through the flow of drums and tamborims and trombones and whistles so that you are momentarily part of it, carried back in it, like jetsam, before piling out on the other side and into the crowd that swallows you up.

Lucy could see the Old Man's top hat thirty yards ahead. She dodged and weaved after it. Twenty yards, fifteen. But each time she made ground, the crowd would thicken and cut her off, as though pushed in her path by the hand of a chess master, cunningly deploying his knights, his bishops and rooks in defence of their cornered king. Lucy would momentarily lose sight of Him – *the boy, the boy*, her lips moved and her eyes shone and her heart beat – and then find him again, forty or fifty yards ahead, his top hat bobbing and breaking cleanly through the crowd in front of the town hall and up Prince Albert Street, along Ship Street, before doubling back toward Meeting House Lane, up Bond Street, up Gardner Street and past the Dorset, the Hand in Hand, down the twitten beside the post office depot and across Queens Road, where Lucy's heart collapsed on its knees when she saw she had lost him altogether. The crowds had lessened when, several streets back, she had left the parade path, but there were still groups of people gathered in front of pubs, and bundles of threes and fours and more puffing along from the train station and the houses uphill, heading toward the seafront and the bonfire and the fireworks or out to meet for Christmas drinks.

Lucy turned in a circle, checking the way she had come and down the snow-sparkling side streets on either side. Nothing. No top hat. The boy was gone. Lucy raised her arms as though in pleading, as though beseeching the night air, and pulling them back in desperation as a shot of icy wind blew downhill. It hit Lucy in the face and pushed her back. When she looked again, she saw the boy a short way uphill, turning down Dorset Street.

But when she got there – it was only just ahead – he was already over a hundred yards away and nearing the far end of the street. Lucy shouted for him to wait, but either he didn't hear or paid no heed. There was no crowd to block her now and Lucy went pelting after the boy.

There were several sets of footprints in the snow, but only one that travelled in the direction the boy was heading. The prints were rhomboidal and had a slender ridge down the middle, as though the soles of his boots were split from toe to arch. At the end of Dorset Street they suddenly leapt left and up the unlit twitten behind the schoolyard. Lucy followed them into Mt Zion Place, where they ran uphill, clean and lone past the church and into Dyke Road. There they stopped dead. Across the street was St Nicholas Gardens, where homeless were known to sleep and where the Old Man, upon His arrival, had robbed the dead man of his clothes. Lucy tried the gates but they had been locked for the night. A bell in the church tower behind her tolled once and low. On instinct, Lucy turned uphill, and found the lone footprints again – the same size, the same shape and distance between steps – and followed them into the ever shadowed twitten, with high flint walls on both sides that ran end to end behind Clifton Gardens (and that tonight smelled of cold stone and ice). She would have seen my prints leading out through the doorway in the twitten wall. I had gone to sit with Sabrina (as though it would somehow keep the two of us warm) and missed Lucy by minutes. If I had been there, I would have warned her, using every inch of body and sound, not to follow His footprints into the garden of No 9, and from the garden indoors, where the Old Man, ravenous and bare, would have fallen to His knees and forearm, one hand stretched back between His pale thighs, scratching and moaning *Home, Home, Home…*

If your story could have been reversed, Lucy, if it could have been folded back on itself, it's there, when you entered the garden, that I would have put the crease. The footprints in the snow, from the moment you followed them up the twitten behind the schoolyard, were always the opposite than how they appeared to you, always the other way around. Not you chasing after the boy, but the Old Man steering you from behind, tight on your heels. So close at times that when He whispered in your ear which direction to go, which footprints to see, you would have felt His cold, coprophagic breath on your face, smelled it so deep in your nose that it would have produced a taste.

The Old Man couldn't keep a tooth in his head. They crumbled and split (and regrew, even more brittle than before) with every song He sang, rotted and dissolved from so little as the touch of His tongue. But He did have one tooth that was sharp and long and strong. And it itched like Hell until He was fed.

I missed you by minutes. I am so sorry.

'Poor old Jarvis. Anyway, Lucy will know what do with him. The Bitch must be full on. She was running round like a madwoman at the Burning of the Clocks the other night. I haven't heard a peep from her since.' Belinda glanced at the wall clock hung in an alcove beside the chimney breast. It was sixteen minutes past four. 'She's in St Lucy mode again, you can tell, but still, she ought to be here by now. I think I'll just text her again and make sure she's all right.' Belinda fetched her phone from where it was charging on top of a stack of books. I couldn't take any more of it and made for the French doors to the little yard at the back. They were locked. I shouted to be let outside. And there, as soon as I was left alone, in the path cleared of snow, I vomited again and again.

Until then the heart-shaped shit had mystified me. It didn't *smell*: it smelled of pure... it had smelled like spring, like a clear, late spring evening. *There be none of Beauty's daughters*, I had thought to myself with its scent filling my nose, *With a magic like thee*. It was whatever love (let's call it what it must have once been) that had somehow grown inside of Him. It was love condemned, love tortured and squeezed. But it was still love. And He had spat (or do I mean shat?) it from His dry lips. It was appalling; I was dazzled.

Belinda's little yard at the back was boxed in on two sides by the flat itself, and on the other two by white-rendered walls festooned with pale lichen and streaky, looping seagull shits. The lower of the two walls was six feet high (the other was at least twice as tall). In my prime, six feet wasn't considered showing off, not by a long chalk. When I was young, six feet was nothing. But now that the brown was beginning to grey, now that I'd grown long of whisker...

Besides, it wasn't only six feet; it was six feet and six inches – the extra half a foot was snow. But I reckoned that wouldn't matter, so long as I managed to dislodge it.

But before I had a chance to properly gauge things, the static-y whine of Belinda's doorbell sounded in the front hall. This was it: I wasn't sticking round. Not with everyone about to clock something had happened to Lucy. Not with me here when Lucy was... It was out the front door or over the wall.

I crouched, concentrated and leapt.

On the other side of the wall was the little backyard of the house next door, and next to it was the little backyard of the house next door but one, with a wall in between. Beyond that, another little yard and another wall, and on and on, stretching out like weeks and seasons in the mindless dark.

If it is possible to love so completely that it fills the whole of you, that you feel it in your blood and lungs, your toes, your spine and in how it charms the words as they lift from your tongue, then perhaps it is possible to hate so completely that it hollows you. And if it can hollow you so completely, then perhaps it is possible that that hollowing becomes unfastened. It not only consumes you, but also empties everything that's near.

I believe that is what happened. I believe that is what happened to Lucy. And what happened to my home.

When I had left 9 Clifton Gardens to sit with Sabrina the night

Lucy chased down the Old Man, I had already eaten dinner and there was no later rendezvous to bear in mind. Time was my own. I went to sit with Sabrina because sentimentality got the better of me. It was the longest night of the year, and one of the coldest. I wanted to keep her company, I wanted to... If I am permitted to say one good thing about myself (not that it affords me any sense of absolution, not that it untacks the dread, the guilt), I will say this: I never stopped loving Sabrina. Not even when she... Even to sit with her in silence was to feel loved – to feel it and to return it. That night I sat on her grave until the church bells chimed an hour had passed. I remembered to her afternoons getting stoned in the sun, games of tag, of hide-and-seek, the Christmas Eve we'd feasted on pheasant before the fire, the way we knew exactly how to nip and needle at each other when we were over-tired. I fed her all the latest gossip from The Glaring and from home. And by the time I returned to Clifton Gardens, the carnage was complete. At first, everything looked as it did when I had left. The *oeil-de-boef* was centred high below the eaves. The knobbly, snow-laden wisteria vines made a jigsaw of the once clean white façade above the back door. The iced over steel shutters were on the windows. The cat flap hung still and mud-stained in the utility room window where the squatters had wrenched the steel shutter away. But when I poked my head indoors, I only just managed to pull up short of going all the way. Inside, where there had been rooms and cupboards and ceilings and floors and a staircase with white spindles and a ruddy-gold railing, where there had been runners and rugs, a piano, pupils, potted plants, parties, food, music and life, there was a hole – and in the hole, the cold, the dark and the damp of the deep. A rancid and ruthless hole; it went down and down and disappeared far below, into a dark mist that turned in the darkness, and in that darkness was a deeper darkness, swallowing everything in sight. Of all that had been the house, the only things that remained were a wall mirror on the second floor that shone black with night and, beneath where the ground floor had been, a long wooden joist. Old, brown and worm-holed, its far end had been sheared off to a savage point.

When I returned indoors from Belinda's little yard at the back, I found Wiggy in my seat. He sat precisely in the middle of the chair, with his hands on its arms and his knees pointing at me. I glared at him and tried to say something. Wiggy clicked his tongue. I farted silently and left the room. In the kitchen I found a plate of fried bacon sandwiched between sheets of kitchen roll and quickly helped myself. Pork had been rarity at home. The Rothenbergs hadn't kept kosher, but because of a reverential and nostalgic observance for their forbears, it was never in ready supply. It was only when one was away visiting friends that the other would indulge – even gorge – on a fry-up that each naively believed the other never suspected, nor took part in themselves. It was funny: both Ernie and Margaret would attempt to buy my silence and abetment with some bacon or a sausage and the same words – 'Mum your maw, Geoffrey Cantor. Mum your maw.' – delivered with a nod a wink and a kiss.

Mum your maw. And now I couldn't speak, when there was so much I ought to say. But the hole, the horror of that hole – I wanted to shield everyone from it, to shield them from even knowing of it, and through muteness defend, however temporarily (an hour, two hours, a day) the effortless jollity they shared right then and that was palpable in their eyes, their loose limbs and in their pops of snorting laughter. But the narrow red wand on the wall clock circled on, counting away the dead seconds, the minutes, as day flew down into night. When after I had returned to the sitting room once more and a lump of a coal fell, still glowing, from the grate, I gave everyone a last look and managed a noise that Anna repeated back to me twice over, adding a question mark at the end. I didn't deign her with a reply and went upstairs and curled up in bed. It smelled of Belinda and was covered in her clothes. But it was wide and it was cosy. I could get used to this, I said to myself. And tucking my nose under my forepaw and laying my tail atop both, I closed my eyes.

Outside, beneath the night sky, are the cold sea and the snow-smoothed swells of the Downs. Brighton lies nestled between, gleaming in the moonlight. Its warmth surrounds me.

Acknowledgement

While this is a work of fiction, Burning the Clocks is an actual and annual Brighton event, since 1994, run by Same Sky, a community arts organisation. To find out more, please visit www.samesky.co.uk

Also by Christopher Chase Walker

Now You Know

COSMIC EGG BOOKS

Cosmic Egg Books

FANTASY, SCI-FI, HORROR & PARANORMAL

If you prefer to spend your nights with Vampires and
Werewolves rather than the mundane then we publish the books
for you. If your preference is for Dragons and Faeries or Angels
and Demons – we should be your first stop. Perhaps your
perfect partner has artificial skin or comes from another planet –
step right this way. If your passion is Fantasy (including magical
realism and spiritual fantasy), Metaphysical Cosmology, Horror
or Science Fiction (including Steampunk), Cosmic Egg books
will feed your hunger. Our curiosity shop contains treasures
you will enjoy unearthing.

If you have enjoyed this book, why not tell other readers by
posting a review on your preferred book site. Recent bestsellers
from Cosmic Egg Books are:

The Zombie Rule Book
A Zombie Apocalypse Survival Guide
Tony Newton
The book the living-dead don't want you to have!
Paperback: 978-1-78279-334-2 ebook: 978-1-78279-333-5

Cryptogram
Because the Past is Never Past
Michael Tobert
Welcome to the dystopian world of 2050, where three lovers are
haunted by echoes from eight-hundred years ago.
Paperback: 978-1-78279-681-7 ebook: 978-1-78279-680-0

Purefinder
Ben Gwalchmai
London, 1858. A child is dead; a man is blamed and dragged
through hell in this Dantean tale of loss, mystery and fraternity.
Paperback: 978-1-78279-098-3 ebook: 978-1-78279-097-6

600ppm
A Novel of Climate Change
Clarke W. Owens
Nature is collapsing. The government doesn't want you to
know why. Welcome to 2051 and 600ppm.
Paperback: 978-1-78279-992-4 ebook: 978-1-78279-993-1

Creations
William Mitchell
Earth 2040 is on the brink of disaster. Can Max Lowrie stop the
self-replicating machines before it's too late?
Paperback: 978-1-78279-186-7 ebook: 978-1-78279-161-4

The Gawain Legacy
Jon Mackley
If you try to control every secret, secrets may end up
controlling you.
Paperback: 978-1-78279-485-1 ebook: 978-1-78279-484-4

Mirror Image
Beth Murray
When Detective Jack Daniels discovers the journal of female
serial killer Sarah he is dragged into a supernatural world,
where people's dark sides are not always hidden.
Paperback: 978-1-78279-482-0 ebook: 978-1-78279-481-3

Moon Song
Elen Sentier
Tristan died too soon, Isoldé must bring him back to finish his
job… to write the Moon Song.
Paperback: 978-1-78279-807-1 ebook: 978-1-78279-806-4

Perception
Alaric Albertsson
The first ship was sighted over St. Louis...and then St. Louis was
gone.
Paperback: 978-1-78279-261-1 ebook: 978-1-78279-262-8

Readers of ebooks can buy or view any of these bestsellers by clicking on the live link in the title. Most titles are published in paperback and as an ebook. Paperbacks are available in traditional bookshops. Both print and ebook formats are available online.

Find more titles and sign up to our readers' newsletter at http://www.johnhuntpublishing.com/fiction.

Follow us on Facebook at https://www.facebook.com/JHPfiction and Twitter at https://twitter.com/JHPFiction.